Scripting the Truth

T.A. Henry

Copyright © 2015 T.A. Henry

All rights reserved.

ISBN: 1517251729
ISBN-13: 978-1517251727

TO MY DARLING P

You believed in, encouraged, and nurtured my
dream when I was ready to abandon it.

ACKNOWLEDGMENTS

Many of the stories invented for this novel were inspired by the true life stories of QAs as told in their biographies.

This novel is a product of Nanowrimo, National Novel Writing Month, a worldwide challenge to write fifty thousand words in 30 days or less.

At every turn I was guided, advised, and had my hand held by the kind members of SnoValley Writes! My gratitude to you all.

CHAPTER ONE

WHERE IT ALL BEGINS

Everyone talked to me strenuously, and at length, about the seriousness of what I was proposing to undertake. I needed to consider the physical difficulties, the uncomfortableness I would surely have to live with, and the likelihood that I would die in service to my country. I argued that my grandfather had served, my father was currently serving, and as a daughter to a Duke who already had two sons, I was fairly ancillary. My father had already turned our country estate, Goodwin, over to the use of the War Department, and they were rapidly building an air field with the available space. After a titled upbringing and all the requisite training that came in an upper crust boarding school, an adventurous attitude was really all I needed to be eminently suited to a position with the Queen Alexandra Imperial Military Nursing Service. I was given military training and advice on how to survive under the conditions I was likely to encounter overseas. I saw duty as a nurse in Africa and then in a humorous twist of fate, I spent a few nights at Goodwin before we launched on Normandy.

With all that talking and advice and training, the one thing no one mentioned was what to do when I got home; when I survived all the difficulties, when in fact I thrived during war. How was I to handle the boredom and monotony of country life after the nonstop excitement and adventure of war? I found myself constantly at loose end; moving from the London house in Grosvenor Square to the West Sussex estate and back again at a moment's whim. I was uncomfortable everywhere. At first, all around me people were celebrating the defeat of the Germans, the end of the war. But slowly they began to move on. To resume their normal lives; or at least the lives they dreamed would be normal while they waited for the war to be over. They didn't understand the war; what those who served had seen or been through because they hadn't seen it. They stayed safe and warm at home. When I heard people talking about the relief to no longer struggle, my brain couldn't process what they meant. With the exception of a few months during the blitz, their struggles involved ration books and the inability to get butter. My struggle had been worlds away from that.

As I sat in the breakfast room sipping my second cup of coffee, gazing out the window at a foggy country morning, in an effort to make the meal stretch as long as possible, to occupy more hours in the day, my father folded his paper forcibly and irritably cleared his throat.

"Yes Father?" I decided to engage with him as yet another way to waste time.

"Your mother and I are concerned."

"Is the new race track giving you problems?" I said a silent prayer that this was about his race track.

"We are concerned about you." My father's tone was distinctly pointed.

"Ah." I shouldn't have engaged. I should have just silently consumed my coffee and enjoyed the view, such as it was.

There was a long pause while I mused and then my father began again with an effort to keep his ire from coming through too clearly. "Ever since your return you have been," he paused, "restless."

I tilted my head in acknowledgment. No reason not to agree with him when he was echoing my own thoughts so succinctly.

"You clearly need something to occupy yourself."

"That would be helpful," I quipped.

"I am glad you see reason. Starting immediately you can assist me in the development of the family racetrack." He sounded quite satisfied with himself.

I snorted before I could help myself.

My father slammed his coffee cup into the saucer and a bit of coffee sloshed out. The footman moved forward immediately to replace the tainted saucer with a clean one.

I took the time he was distracted to formulate a new answer. "While I appreciate the offer of such enlightened work, I don't think it would suit me."

"Suit you? Would you care to clarify what you do mean by that?" My father's irritation was mounting.

"I've not yet found my footing since my return." I spun out the sentence slowly.

"That is the point at hand young lady." Exasperation rang through.

I sighed deeply; clearly retreat was indicated. "Father, will you give me one week? If I have not found something to do by then I will assist you with the family project."

My father fiddled with his paper, a sure sign that he was bluffing in his consideration. I wondered briefly if his troops had picked up on that. He nodded sharply and sternly replied, "One week then." He stood and left the room in an effort to maintain his composure.

I sighed, poured another cup of coffee, and stared out into the grey morning wondering what I could possibly find to occupy myself in the next week. Clearly a trip back to London was in order. It was time to employ a little out of sight, out of mind. Perhaps if I didn't return home for a few weeks my father would lose sight of this ridiculous idea that I would be of any use building a race track. I could not imagine what skills he thought I could employ to assist him. Perhaps if one of the men got injured I could dress their wounds, but they weren't even to the actual construction phase yet.

CHAPTER TWO

WHERE I ESCAPE

Leaving my third coffee of the morning unfinished, I headed upstairs to begin packing my things. On the way I asked Wadsworth, our butler, to check the train schedule to London for me and send one of the house maids up with the information. She would probably be shocked to find I was packing for myself, but after five and half years on my own I had trouble adjusting back to having things done for me. It still bothered me how much clothing, shoes, and accessories were required to keep up appearances now. I longed for my comfortable khaki trousers. I quickly folded skirt after skirt and button down blouse after blouse. I was already tired of stockings and heels. The impossibility of living anything approaching a functional life and keeping your seams straight had driven me to the brink of distraction more than once since my return.

I was just closing the lid of my valise when the maid knocked gently and then entered. "The next London bound train leaves in just over an hour milady."

"Thank you Beatrice."

"Might I assist you with your packing, milady?"

"No thank you. I've finished. If you will just let Charles know I will need a ride to the train station in a few minutes."

Beatrice curtsied, "Yes, milady."

I slung my valise off the bed and started for the door.

"Excuse me, milady," Beatrice reached for the luggage.

"I have it, thank you." I gave her a stern look to go with my polite tone.

With a slight huff she flounced down the stairs in search of our chauffeur.

I left my valise in the front hall and headed in search of my parents. I located my father in the study with his pet architect poring over the design paperwork. "I'm off to London by the eleven o'clock train, Father."

"Come in and look at the brilliant ideas Aiden has suggested. Tell me what you think."

I sighed and considered whether it was worth another argument. In the end the onus of time demanded I be quick with my praise and get out. I crossed to the drafting table.

Aiden Jenner smiled shyly at me. "Good morning to you Miss Margaret."

"Good morning." I glanced down at the papers which seemed a mass of confusion to my untrained eye. "Brilliant."

My father looked at me with a narrow eye but I smiled sweetly and bid him farewell. As I headed back to the door my father called out, "Do not think I have forgotten our deal already. One week."

I paused but chose discretion as the better part of valor.

Striding quickly across the house I located my mother in her sun room with a copy of Vogue newly sent airmail from across the pond. "I'm heading back to London by the eleven fifteen."

Her slight startle revealed how absorbed by the new fashions she was. "Already, darling? You just came down by the four forty yesterday."

I started to reply but she continued before I could decide on my defensive strategy.

"Your father and I wanted to talk to you." Her voice held a plaintive note.

"Yes, I know. We discussed things this morning."

"Do not take on so. We just want to see you settled. Married perhaps?"

I kept my tone light. "Not a man on the horizon I'm afraid."

"There could be if you were not so flighty. Stay down here. The hunting season will be starting soon. All the eligible bachelors of proper station will be spending huge swaths of time in the neighborhood."

I ground my teeth to keep from telling her what I thought of men of a proper station. "I'll come back down.

You let me know when the situation is promising." I smiled and hoped this would be enough to get me out the door.

Her excitement immediately went up a notch. "That is a wonderful idea. Why don't I arrange a weekend shooting party? When shall we?"

I wanted to put the brakes on this out of control disaster but she was moving forward at a spitfire pace.

Swinging her legs off the edge of the fainting couch she strode across to her writing desk to consult the calendar there. "Three weeks you think? Or maybe four? I think four weeks to make sure I can really guarantee a good attendance. I'll pencil that in."

I swallowed hard. How to tell my mother this was not at all what I had meant. It was beyond impossible. Brigadier General Wingate always said we could do the impossible in a day but miracles took a bit longer. And this needed a miracle. It was time for me to bow out quickly. I could take my time in London to work out the details of my permanent escape from the safety of distance. "I must dash to make the train. Charles is waiting with the car."

My mother crossed quickly to me and placed a kiss on my cheek. I allowed the embrace and briefly hugged her back, if one could call it a hug when you placed your hands on someone's arms and mentally restrained yourself from shoving them bodily away from you.

I breathed a big sigh of relief as I slid into the back of the Rolls Royce Silver Wraith. "Drive Charles and be quick about it. I can't miss this train."

"Yes milady." Charles nodded his understanding.

As we rolled out the gates I felt tension start to ebb from my shoulders. I would have liked to imagine my mother meant well. But I knew what was best for me was the last thing on her mind. She was only acting according to what she knew, to the dictates of her world. Marry off your daughter and marry her off well. I was her only daughter. My war service had been a huge strain on her, so far was it from her idea of appropriate behavior for someone of my status. My brothers went at the first sign of trouble and although she cried she was proud. I couldn't understand why I should be any different. We just lived in different worlds, with rules as far apart as the Sun and Moon. By the time I finished these musings we were pulling up to the station in Portsmouth. I would catch the London express here.

Charles lifted my valise out of the trunk and cocked his upraised fingers for a porter. Despite the enormous size of the station, located on a main port with tourists, goods shipments, and mail station, a porter appeared immediately to take my luggage. The prestige that came with a title did have its benefits even as it was cloying in its protective rules of etiquette. "Thank you Charles."

He tipped his hat. "My lady."

I slipped into the first class carriage and was blissfully alone. No one was traveling this morning. It was an odd time, too late for businessmen, and few people could afford the cost of a first class ticket. This brought me to the issue at hand. What was I going to do? I needed to find some occupation that would satisfy my father without offending my mother. My mind was blank. I didn't want to go back into a civvy hospital. After so much freedom the idea of being under the thumb of an oppressive matron with curfews and strict codes of conduct, sharing a house with other nurses, made me shudder. I'd rather work on the race track. For the next hour and a half I considered everyone I had known before the war and what, if anything, I knew they were doing now. I really had become quite isolated. I pulled out my notepad and jotted down a few thoughts so I would feel I accomplished something for all my musing.

CHAPTER THREE

WHERE I MEET AN OLD FRIEND

The next evening found me venturing out in the London fog to meet Lila O'Rourke, an old true friend from Stonecroft, my boarding school, at a Chelsea coffee bar. She conveyed her thrill to see me with a squeal the moment I walked in. I smiled and tried to avoid her effusive hug as I shrugged off my coat and peeled off my gloves.

"Darling, where have you been moldering?" Dramatic as ever, Lila still spoke as though she were in West End before an audience of hundreds.

"Here and there."

"How long since you were, released or whatever they call it? Released makes it sound like you were in gaol." Lila said with a laugh.

I couldn't help but chuckle a little at this. "It's called being demobbed, Lila." At her puzzled face I continued, "Short for demobilized."

Comprehension finally dawned. "Yes, that."

"A few months. I had finished my five years and stayed on just a bit to oblige."

"Wasn't it just dreary over there?"

I shrugged, hoping to talk of something else. "Glad to see the Blitz didn't dampen your spirits."

"It would take a good deal more than a few huns to break me. We can take it." She gave a bright smile as she mimicked the posters that used to hang on every flat surface in London by swinging a fist upward toward her opposite shoulder.

I smiled at the catch phrase which had been so thrown about during the war. "What are you doing now?"

"Oh darling, it's dreadful. I simply go from party to party trying not to be married off by my mother and yet desperately heart broken when the bachelor of the day doesn't seem interested in little old me." She fluttered her eyelashes and placed one hand on her chest.

Laughter burst out of me. "I find myself in a similar situation, minus the parties and the heartbreak."

"Don't you want to get married?" Lila queried, as though I was a new species she had not encountered before and wanted desperately to figure out.

"Not particularly. But I have got to find something to do."

"The old man didn't lose all his money in the war did he?" Her eyebrows nearly rose into her victory curl at this outrageous thought.

"No, the Duke is still well and happily rolling in it but he thinks I need to settle down."

"Ah. Fathers." Lila shook her head and paused while I gave the waitress my order. She suggested a few nibbles, to which I nodded my acquiescence so she would go away.

"Lila, this is serious. My father is threatening to make me work on his raceway design plan if I don't find something to do in the next week."

"How ghastly. Doesn't he have a proper architect?"

"He does. And I think said architect has a bit of a crush which makes the whole thing so much more…"

We both sighed and sipped our coffee. With her free hand Lila tapped out a little *Etude on Table Top*.

"Ok, I've got it. Go to work in a hospital." Lila's voice oozed with pleasure at own her suggestion.

"Don't you think I've thought of that? I couldn't stand it. All the strict rules and moral codes. Too much after the years of delicious freedom."

"Delicious freedom? That's it then."

I shook my head as once again Lila's train of thought had left the station without me, possibly without Lila as well.

"Isn't there some way you could keep being a QA?"

"I suppose I could join the regulars." I frowned, considering the possibility.

"Oh dear, is that what they call it? Sounds so… milk delivery."

"Nothing could be further from the truth. I don't know though. Maybe I will mark that down as a last ditch possibility."

The aforementioned nibbles were delivered and we snacked in between thinking and gossiping about old friends. We wrapped things up rather soon as Lila had dinner and dancing plans she needed to prepare for. We had walked only a short way together when Lila gestured at a movie poster in front of a theatre, and asked, "Have you seen the new Rank film, yet?"

I shook my head as my eyes followed her hand. I stopped dead on the pavement. Lila stopped a moment later and turned to see what had my attention. "Oh I know. Isn't he dreamy?"

I nodded but couldn't speak. I had seen those eyes before; I knew it was not just the black and white print that made them appear grey but that they really were a cool grey of London fog when it was thick and enveloping. I had cared for the soldier who belonged to them for fifty-eight hours. He had left with my heart. With great difficulty I resumed walking but could muster little to say as Lila chattered about her plans and made suggestions as to procuring me invitations to future events. I finally stopped her by hugging her briefly and thanking her for meeting me.

Her eyes narrowed. "You have that look. Something is going on in that mind of yours. Care to share?"

I smiled but shook my head. I needed desperately to be alone so I could figure out how to meet my soldier again.

CHAPTER FOUR

WHERE THE GAME IS AFOOT

By the following morning I had concocted a plan. I dressed in my favorite Schiaparelli suit for the aura of professionalism it lent my visage, which I desperately needed if I was going to pull off the plan I had in mind. I rang for a cab to drive me to the Lime Grove Studio, timing my arrival for mid-morning in hopes that most of the office staff would be having their elevenses and I could successfully parry with a lesser office being. Sadly, there was but an office boy in total at Lime Grove. I moved onto Islington as the next closest office of Rank Organization. Here I struck pay dirt. The office was busy despite it being almost upon the sacred lunch hour. I straightened my beret, checked my lipstick, and powdered my nose before tackling the gargoyle in charge.

"I have business with Patrick Dumount. Please let him know Lady Margaret Leighton is here to see him." I hoped my no nonsense verbiage combined with my most brisk tone would get me past the first hurdle.

"You have business do you?" The woman's tone was designed to mock. I got a little nervous.

"I do." Simple and direct. Act as though there is no reason she shouldn't do exactly what I wanted her to do. That was the trick.

"I'll bet. You must be the ninth girl this week who tried the business sham to get to see Patrick, and the 200th since that film hit the box office. Now be off with you before I call security."

"Oh but I know Patrick. I am sure if you told him Lady Margaret Leighton was here he would want to see me."

"Listen sweetheart pretending to be nobility is actually an offense punishable by law. So take yourself off now."

"My father really is the Duke of Richmond and I am Lady Leighton and I need to see Patrick Dumount on urgent business." I found myself getting a bit short in the temper.

"Tell you what honey, bring the good Duke down here and then maybe I'll believe your story." With that she picked up her phone and began to slowly push buttons. "I'm calling the security officer right now. I'd be long gone before he arrives if I were you."

Unless I was prepared to involve my father in this mess I had no choice but to retire bested. As I slowly made my way to the door a flyer on the cork board caught my eye.

"Actresses wanted. Must speak proper English, ride to the hounds, and know how to play the harpsichord."

I grabbed the page off the wall and shoved it under the eye of the gargoyle. "I wish to audition."

The woman sighed, shook her head, and began dialing again.

"No, really. I want to audition. Don't call security," I panicked.

"Not dialing security this time. The fastest way to get rid of you is to send you over to talent and let them kick you out."

I considered a scathing retort but again discretion is the better part of valor so I merely smiled sweetly and took a seat to wait for my escort. It was close on twenty five minutes when an out of breath young woman in slacks and a head scarf rushed through the door. "Where is she?"

The gargoyle gestured to me. The young woman took one look at me and snorted. "Come on then."

I followed her breakneck pace as we wove in between buildings heading only she knew where. Finally she whipped open a door and whirled through, whispering "not a peep" to me from over her shoulder. I followed her into a small sound stage where a young woman was demonstrating her ability on the harpsichord. I grimaced. I hadn't expected to have to play. I hadn't touched a harpsichord since I left finishing school. I was bound to be rusty to put it lightly. My guide gestured me over to a row of chairs, most of which were occupied by young women. I was thinner than some, plumper than others. Prettier than some and wow, very much the ugly duckling compared to a few. And I couldn't play the harpsichord. I needed to get a part so I could have access to the film studio and find Patrick on my own. But things did not look promising.

Finally the young woman shouted, "New girl, up on stage."

I gestured to myself and she nodded, "Come on you, we don't have all day."

I cleared my throat and removed my hat and gloves leaving them behind on my chair, along with my clutch.

"Where's your card?"

I stepped back to the chair and grabbed my bag pulling out a calling card, handing it to the girl who had guided me here. She laughed and shook her head. "Your shot card." I looked at her puzzled. "Your stats card?" Still puzzled. She sighed, "You don't have any clue do you?"

"Um, no."

"Fine, fine. Just go up there."

I stood quietly in the middle of the stage with my hands folded in front of me. I could see very little of the people in the room. The lights were not full house down but the stage brights were definitely in my eyes.

A man bellowed, "Name."

I hesitated, better to be casual here. "Molly Leighton."

"Age?"

"Twenty eight." Hadn't he been told it was really impolite to ask a lady her age.

"You can ride to the hounds and play the harpsichord?"

"Yes."

"Experience?"

"Experience?" I had no clue what he was asking. Did he want to know how often I rode to the hounds. Or how often I questioned so rudely by strange men.

"What have you acted in?" He spoke each word so slowly it was obvious he thought I was dim.

"Just the occasional family production at Christmas."

I heard muffled laughter from throughout the room. Well really, if you had a large pile of stones in the country and a lot of family that descended for the holidays, you put on plays to fight off boredom while snowed in, which inevitably happened every year between Boxing Day and New Year.

"Yes, well, thank you."

I raised an eyebrow and waited. And waited. After two minutes the man looked up from his papers. "That was your dismissal." His tone held a hint of laughter restrained.

"I see. Thank you."

As I collected my belongings the girl guide reappeared to escort me out. "I suppose this means I didn't make the grade?"

She smiled, not unkindly, and shook her head. "Afraid not. The complete lack of experience is a bit of a stumbling block."

"Well thank you anyway. You don't have to walk me out, I can find my way."

"Nice of you to offer but it is procedure."

Inwardly I groaned. There was simply no catching a break for Patrick and I. I started trying to puzzle out a new method to get free reign of this film complex. With half an ear I was listening to my girl guide prattle on about the complications of her job when I caught her mentioning something about the director looking for new film scripts. I paused in my step and half turned to face her, catching her arm. "Scripts?"

She laughed. "Do you have any experience with films?"

"Not really no." I laughed at myself a bit.

"So the director who was just auditioning actresses?" She paused and I nodded. "He is looking for a new script to make a new movie." She spoke slowly as though explaining things to a small child. I didn't mind though because she gave me a brilliant idea.

"And how would one submit a film script for consideration?"

She gave me a searching glance. "You could contact me. Elizabeth Barrow." She paused and held out her hand to shake mine.

"Molly Leighton." I took her hand and gave it a solid squeeze. "I'll bring something in to you then." I smiled broadly, almost giddy with delight.

Her glance said she'd believe it when she saw it but I didn't give a toss. I could write a script. It couldn't be that hard. I picked up my pace as we headed for the exit, eager to get home and start assembling a script.

CHAPTER FIVE

WHERE I DISCOVER HOW HARD IT CAN BE TO WRITE

I grabbed a cab to save time. While the driver negotiated London traffic for my return home, I pondered a topic for my script. I only really knew two things. The life afforded me by my noble birth with boarding schools, country homes, and short trips abroad, or the war. Writing about my upbringing seemed so immodest, almost like I was bragging about where I came from and who I knew. It seemed to me that people would be much more interested in true tales from the war we had just won at great cost. I could pen some sort of homage to the sacrifice and bravery of those who served. That I could do. That I could write. Then I wondered how long the script should be, I typed 60 words a minute. Maybe I could have something done by Friday. I rang up Lila the second I got home.

Flighty though she was, Lila had always been my partner in crime while we were away to school together.

"I have a plan but I need your help," I announced without preamble.

"Of course darling."

"Do you know anyone in the film business?"

"Film." There was a long pause. "Are you thinking about being an actress? A job in rep might be a better place to start."

Laughing, I explained I had already tried the actress route and things had gone rather pear shaped. "So now I need to write a film script, preferably by the weekend. But I don't know much about the process."

"Oh my. The things you do before tea time. I do know someone who could help. Let me call her and see if I can set up a meeting."

"Today." Nothing ventured, nothing gained.

"Molly, today might be asking a bit too much."

"Today, Lila, today. I have to get this script going," I insisted.

"So start writing and then you can adjust after you talk to my friend."

I sat silent and stunned for a moment. Sometimes scatter brained friends really came up with the simplest ideas that hit it bang on.

"Are you still there?" Lila queried.

"I am stunned into silence by your brilliance."

Lila laughed. "Go on then. Ring you back shortly."

"Ta."

I rummaged around in my father's library to find his old corona typewriter. I lifted the dust cover and prayed for a fresh tape. I rolled in a piece of paper and tried a few keys. It seemed in working order but the tape was shot. I rang the bell via a button on the side of my father's desk. Thirty seconds later the lower house maid entered and curtsied. "I need a new typewriter ribbon. I have pulled out the old one so you can get the right thing. Please go out now and get me one immediately."

As per her training she merely bobbed and took the tape, no doubt muttering about my insanity in her own mind. I cared not. I would hand write until she got back. I grabbed a pencil and a stack of paper and sat down to compose. Where to start my opus?

Several minutes later I had sharpened my pencil, drawn a little sketch of a QA in her cape on the corner of my page, and commenced pacing the floor. I pushed the button to ring the bell again. The same housemaid answered in the same thirty seconds. "Alice, you're back. Wonderful. Where's my ribbon tape?"

"Begging your pardon my lady but Quinten sent one of the gardeners."

"Oh. Yes, I see. I would like a cup of coffee and a sandwich served to me here please."

She bobbed and withdrew from the room.

Perhaps food would provide some spark of intelligence. Why was this so hard? I had lived the war. Surely I knew what happened and could put it down on paper. Maybe I should just start with my time waiting at Goodwin before we landed at Normandy. Did I need to write it chronologically? Could I just start sketching out scenes on paper and then arrange them into a continuous story later? Yes, yes, I would try that.

My coffee and sandwich came. I paused to eat and ponder. I could start with the simplest details first. Perhaps the bits that might surprise the average viewer of the final movie? Or maybe with the biggest shocks? No, no, there would be time for that later. So on to the easy part.

Our leading lady is sent to Harrods to outfit herself in uniform. The list is long and specific and the government grant she receives covers only half the expense. This is perhaps part of the government's plan to ensure only young ladies of reasonably good breeding are chosen to the profession. Each QA would outfit herself with 4-5 ward dresses, a walking out suit and hat, a grey mess dress, a starched lawn cap which must hang to mid back in a sharp point, a tropical kit which included an all-white overall, stockings, and shoes. Not to be forgotten was the trademark grey cape with red trim. The kit included a tin trunk for holding all the above, plus a camp bed, bed roll, canvas wash bowl with tripod, collapsible canvas bath, canvas bucket, and a Beatrice paraffin stove.

In 1936 when many fully trained nurses were receiving their mobilization orders, complete with travel warrants to their units from anywhere in the country, I was just beginning my days as a trainee nurse. It took four years of ward work under a demanding matron before you could enlist. I admit much of my time was more pleasant than for most girls. A title has that effect on the matron of the local hospital, where your home is the grandest in the surrounding countryside and your family holds fetes in honor of said hospital.

I was assigned to the 67th British General Hospital in Phillippeville to support Operation Torch. It was a long sailing from Southampton to Africa through the Mediterranean, which was heavily patrolled by German U-boats. We traveled in a convoy for most of the way, which gave little solace in the long run, as we had been told before we boarded that if one ship in the convoy got hit the others would continue on. No survivors would be picked up from the water without special instructions from on high. On the other hand, as commissioned Lieutenants we QA's got officer's quarters, in what had been first class on the luxury liner before it was requisitioned by the Royal Navy, and officer's mess on the ship. No rationing of food in that dining hall I assure you. As nice as the cabins were, we weren't allowed to close our doors at night in case we did get torpedoed and the ship warped, jamming the doors and trapping us inside as the ship sunk. Sadly the Navy had learned this the hard way and several QAs had drowned on previous sailings when their cabin doors jammed.

My ship was indeed sunk in the Med on the way to my posting. Everyone who did not die in the immediate torpedo incident was picked up and survived but all of our hospital gear was lost to Davy Jones. We nurses were sent to live in Colonial Villas that had been abandoned since the start of the war in Africa. It was beautiful quarters but most were completely empty. Cold marble was our share more often than we liked to talk about.

With Operation Torch we saw so many men coming from the battlefields with injuries each bed was often occupied by three different men per day. We were fairly well stocked; we even had penicillin which was not available in civvy hospitals when I had left England. We had facilities for minor surgery only, an amputation or to set a fracture, before we transferred them to hospital ship. Gangrene was our biggest foe.

It took me better than two hours to write this short bit. I had seriously underestimated the magnitude of this undertaking. Thankfully I was interrupted by the return of the housemaid with the much needed carbon tape. I could abandon wrestling with my literary ambitions and begin wrestling with the physical manifestations of writing this screen play. Halfway through that torturous process the phone rang. I could have left it for the one of the staff to answer but I was desperate to hear back from Lila.

"Darling?"

"Lila. Thank god. This is turning out to be much harder than I thought. Please tell me you have secured me some help."

With rancorous laughter she told me to be at her club for tea at five thirty that afternoon "and do not be late. Marlene is very aware of her own importance, in her mind, anyway. You should be as well."

With a laugh and then an exclamation as to the time, I rang off. I dashed upstairs to my room to change into an appropriate outfit. I was halted by the sight of myself in the mirror over the wash stand. It appeared I had gotten carbon all over the side of my face while speaking with Lila. I sighed and rang for warm water. When it came I asked the house maid to order me a taxi.

I scrubbed myself vigorously and then applied extra powder to cover the blackish grey stain I could not quite get off the side of my face. Rummaging through my hats I looked for something I could wear to shield that side. In the back of my wardrobe, I found a cloche from the early thirties; I must have worn it to a costume party at some point with a flapper ensemble. It would do today since it pushed my hair forward covering the smudges. I grabbed a silky shirt dress and tried to straighten my stockings. How I longed for my trousers. Low heel lace up shoes and a swing coat completed the vaguely old fashioned look. Just enough that it nodded to a more playful time. Not as though I was a provincial miss.

My taxi was waiting as I rushed down the stairs. "The Savage Club, 1 Carlton House Terrace please."

It was only ten or twelve blocks, but required going past Piccadilly Circus, and that was always a nightmare no matter the time of day. The drive took the twenty minutes I had estimated and six more. I rushed up the stairs.

CHAPTER SIX

WHERE I AM FORCED TO BE HONEST

I was late but once I crossed the threshold I slowed to an appropriate pace. The director raised an eyebrow and immediately came out from behind his centuries old and polished to within an inch of it's life mahogany desk, to direct me to the ladies waiting room. Savage was still an old boys club but they did allow women to have tea on the premises if their husbands or fathers were full members. The room was almost deserted, other than Lila and the older lady sitting with her. There was one other occupied table containing a mother and daughter pair clearly shopping for the afternoon and stopping to refresh themselves before they caught the train home to one of the fashionable outlying suburbs of London with three golf courses and a good commuter train for the men to travel by each day. This was the life my mother wanted for me. She would give her Vogue subscription to be sitting here with me planning our joint Christmas spectacle dinner and chiding me to provide an heir as soon as possible. I shook my head gently to clear these troublesome thoughts and moved to Lila, who was gesturing at me as though it was a crowded tube platform. She rose and kissed me on both cheeks as I slipped off my coat. A servant appeared immediately to whisk it away to the coat closet.

"This is the renowned Marlene Dupree."

I bobbed a short curtsy, which seemed to be enough to mollify her irritation at my tardiness. "It is a great pleasure to meet you."

She smiled as though this was her due. "We've ordered without you."

I smiled and laughed inwardly at her lack of breeding. I was one minute late and they had ordered without me. No matter, I wasn't here to eat but to acquire a bit of knowledge to help me get closer to seeing Patrick again.

Lila laughed at the awkwardness of her friend and tried to smooth the way. "Marlene, Molly is writing a screen play and could use some of your amazing advice garnered from your years of experience."

Marlene narrowed her eyes. I don't think she liked the reference to the number of years. She was definitely a touch long in the tooth. I briefly wondered what her real name was. I imagined the fun I would have with Lila later puzzling that out.

"I have spent some time in the film industry as well as on stage."

I nodded sagely as though I understood. "Do tell me anything you can."

Marlene cleared her throat and was obviously preparing to deliver a lecture when the tea service arrived. She leaned back in her chair with a frown and waited. I poured to oblige, wondering if I could take a sandwich while I listened or if she would find that rude. I slowly reached out to take a tea cake. Marlene either did not notice or was not irritated by the action.

"When writing a script you must consider your audience as well as who might be best suited to play each character. You have to give some thought to the cost of production as every studio will want to make a film as cheaply as possible to optimize their return on investment. Snappy dialog is a must no matter which genre you are writing for. Do not add too much direction otherwise the director will feel like you are trying to do his job and nothing irritates a director like not being able to act like God. Are you following me?"

I nodded, actually rapt with attention. Dialog? Return on investment? Actors? All I knew was I wanted to spend time with Patrick.

"Who are you writing for?"

"My audience you mean? Or which studio? This script is for Rank Organization."

"Which director at Rank?"

I paused. I didn't know his name.

Marlene immediately picked up my uncertainty. "Has this script been commissioned?"

I shook my head.

Marlene sighed deeply and threw an unrecognizable look at Lila. Lila smiled in return and reached forward placing a hand on Marlene's. "If anyone can help Molly it is you."

There was a long pause as I poured more tea in Marlene's cup. Marlene struck a pose, staring off into space above the fireplace. I waited. Lila smiled at me. I absentmindedly grabbed a sandwich, cucumber, and I hated cucumber, but I ate it anyway.

The haughty tone disappeared as Marlene leaned forward to me. "Alright. Let's get down to brass tacks. What have you written?"

"I didn't really even know what a script should have so I started writing just bits from my service."

"Exposition?"

I blinked. "I do not understand what you are asking me."

With another sigh Marlene began to lecture again. "A film script should be almost entirely dialog. You can have some exposition writing that explains a setting and some actions. But eighty to ninety percent will be dialog. This means you need to explain everything that happens, everything people are thinking, their motivations through conversation with others. You can use some exposition to tell the actors what their character is thinking or feeling."

My stomach sunk. "All exposition so far." I tried to sound upbeat but dismay was cold and clammy around my heart.

"I see. You will simply have to start again. A good way to work it out is to pretend you are talking to a friend. Write down what you would say if you were telling her a story. Imagine what she would say in return."

I nodded. "I can do that," I said with more trepidation than when I signed to go to war.

"Why are you so desperate to do this?" Marlene asked simply and I got the impression she actually cared to know what my answer might be.

"I met this man. He was a soldier. I nursed him. He's an actor now for Rank and I… this is the only way I can get to see him again."

Lila set down her tea cup with a thump and a slosh. "My God Molly, have you finally fallen in love?"

I smiled sheepishly.

Lila threw herself back in her chair and pretended to fan her face with her hand. "The shock, my heart."

I laughed uproariously and to my surprise Marlene joined. We shared a genuine smile.

"Thank you Marlene. Truly."

"I could take a look if you like, after you get a bit down on paper."

"I don't want to impose upon your time."

Marlene waved my words away. "You and my goddaughter have been friends a long time. It is the least I can do for her and by extension for you."

I smiled. It made such perfect sense to me that Lila should have an actress godmother.

"I'll give you a ring over the weekend then."

Lila tapped my arm, "Let's have lunch Saturday and go shopping. We could catch up more and talk out any plot issues you have."

I laughed but agreed, after all Lila had just kept me from making a total fool of myself when I went to submit my script. The least I could do was grant her a few hours of shopping time.

CHAPTER SEVEN

WHERE I WRITE IN EARNEST

While I walked home all sorts of memories returned to me. I arrived on the front step in a flush of inspiration. Speeches made by training officers and matrons. Crazy little conversations I had with fellow QAs. I was eager to get them on paper before they flew out of my brain and were lost.

Entering the house I threw off my coat into the arms of Quinten, the butler, and rushed straight back to the library. My papers had been straightened up and the new ribbon tape successfully installed in the typewriter. A sheet of paper had been rolled in and aligned for me. Quinten had followed me into the room after handing my coat off to the upper housemaid who would hang it in my closet.

I tossed my gloves, clutch, and hat into a chair. "Is this your good work Quinten?"

"Yes, my lady."

"Thank you. I shall be holed up in this room for the immediate future. It could be days. Please have food sent in regularly and keep a supply of hot coffee constantly at the ready for me to imbibe as needed."

"Yes, my lady."

I nodded my dismissal and moved around the desk to sit in the chair in front of the typewriter. Quinten had not left the room as befitted the well trained servant he was. "Is there something more?"

"His lordship rang this evening while you were out."

I sighed, and then rallied. "I have no time for phone calls now or in the immediate future. Tell my callers I am in bed with typhus if you must but do not disturb me for anything short of a German invasion."

"Yes, my lady."

This time Quinten exited the room and I was momentarily grateful for the reality of well-trained servants. Then I turned my attention to the task at hand.

Scene In:

Twenty-two young and not so young budding QAs listening with rapt attention to the matron.

"Ladies, you must understand you will be outnumbered by hundreds of men to each young lady. They will be charming. They will be daring. Many will be married. Take great care to choose your companions carefully. Getting involved with a married man is always a dangerous and potentially deadly idea."

One QA whispers to another. "Deadly? What the wife will track you down in theater and kill you?" The other QA giggles.

Despite her whispering the matron has heard her. "Imagine yourself pregnant, homeless, abandoned by the baby's father, barred from your profession, and friendless because who would associate herself with someone so low. Death is the only option left to one who has placed herself in such a situation."

The QAs struggle not to snicker.

The door had opened noiselessly and I found a tray with dinner at my elbow. Pheasant, stuffing, braised Brussels sprouts, Stilton cheese and crackers. "I can't possibly eat this while typing. Take it away and bring me something easy to consume with one hand."

Quinten nodded and removed the tray.

Scene In:

Canvas mess tent in the North African desert at Phillippeville. Small bar set up in the corner. Tables scattered around on sand floor.

QAs milling around with Officers they have invited. Clock on the wall should read 8:45, it is night.

Lead: "Are you really planning to go back with him?"

Friend: "Sure. They have to leave here in the next fifteen minutes per the dragoness and the night is still young."

Both glance at the matron who with pursed lips is working on paperwork in the corner of the tent, keeping an eye on her girls.

Lead: "Curfew is eleven. If you're late you know what it means."

Friend: "I can go and be back. The Yanks have beer and movies."

Lead: "I've heard they have a lot more than that."

Both girls giggle.

Friend: "I might take advantage of that as well."

Lead: "Be careful. A condom isn't the answer to every problem. He's a Yank and from all I hear they are rarely serious in their attentions."

Friend: "Who said I was looking for serious? You worry too much. See you at curfew."

Scene Out

Scene In

Villa bedroom, lead character in bed, lights out. Knock on the door.

Lead: "Come in."

Other QA: "Friend hasn't come back yet and it's after curfew. Do you know where she was going tonight?"

Lead: Stumbles to answer not wanting to give her friend away. "I'm not sure."

Other: "If she has to give her name at the gate…."

Lead nods and turns over pretending to go back to sleep but after Other QA closes the door she gets up and goes to look out the window at the empty yard behind the already closed, manned, and gunned gates.

Scene Out

Scene In

Breakfast in the same mess tent. All the QAs except Friend present and eating. All whispering amongst themselves. Matron enters and commands attention.

"Friend has been posted. She is packing now. This means a rearrangement to the schedule. I will have today's changes for you at the end of breakfast."

Lead leaves the tent in search of Friend. She finds her in her room packing.

Friend: "I suppose you heard."

Lead: "Do you know where?"

Friend: "They didn't say but I am to go today in just a few hours."

Lead: "I'm so sorry to have you go." Moves to hug Friend.

Friend: "Just lucky for me he's a Yank so they didn't know he was married or it would be much worse."

Lead: "But still to leave all your friends and him on a moment's notice." Emphasis on the him.

Friend: "If I write a quick note, could you give it to him when he next comes looking for me?"

Lead: "Of course. But you'll have to be quick; I need to be on ward in just a few minutes."

Friend pulls out paper and sits down to write.

Lead: "I'll come back before I go to the ward. I'll just run to my room to get ready."

Friend nods, left writing her goodbye. Lead exits door.

Scene Out

Scene In:

Lead opens door to Friend's room: "Have you got that note ready for me?"

Friend hands it over with a hug. "You might learn from my mistake." Said kindly with a wry smile.

Lead raises eyebrows: "I just might." With similar smile back.

They hug and Lead heads off to the ward.

Tented ward in lines behind the villas. At first show just a few tents and then pull back to show the mass of tents. Follow nurse until she enters a tent.

Scene Out

CHAPTER EIGHT

WHERE I GIVE MYSELF A STOMACH ACHE

I came out of my trance a few hours later with a cup of cold coffee next to the typewriter and a plate of sandwiches at my elbow. Quinten had returned at some point with finger sandwiches, cut small and each made with a gooey center that would hold the bites together so I could write with one hand and eat with the other. Given the half empty plate and my vague stomach ache; I had clearly been munching on them for some time. It was just after eleven. I poured a new cup of coffee and stretched my back. Leaning back in the chair I cradled my coffee cup, sipping and thinking. I wanted to demonstrate some of what happened in the tents but how much could they film? I had no idea. Maybe I should just write it and let the director figure it out.

Scene In:

Lead approaching a bed with a tray. Bottle of powder, mask, and distribution straw. She sets down the tray and leans over to talk to the patient.

Lead: "I need to administer your penicillin now." Said brusquely but not unkindly.

Lead puts on the mask, attaching insufflator. She adds some of the powder. She gently pulls back the bandage on the chest and puffs to distribute penicillin into the wound. Lead jumps slightly shocked and steps back at the sight of his lung rising and falling just where she was placing the penicillin via the insufflator. Shaking her head at her own ridiculousness, she resumes her work, then rebandages the wound.

The Doctor comes by as she is finishing.

Lead: "I've just finished his nine o'clock dose of penicillin."

Doctor nods sharply.

Lead: "I saw, I saw his lung moving while I was puffing the medicine into his chest, should that have happened?"

Doctor nods: "This one isn't likely to make it. The damage is very great. The next twelve hours will tell."

Lead: "Yes Doctor."

Doctor: "Thank you, Sister."

Lead picks up the tray and moves off to the end of the tent to replace the supplies.

Scene Out

Scene In:

Ambulance arriving, driving fast, pulls up hard outside the triage tent. Orderlies meeting the ambulance and offloading multiple patients, blood and gore on all of them. Lead and other QAs rushing to the ready at the front of the tent. Each following a different patient as they are brought in and placed in beds. Lead goes to man who is quite a mess. A doctor rushes up brusquely removing torn and bloodied clothes so he can diagnose the issue.

Doctor: "This man needs immediate surgery. I'll have to amputate that arm. Prep him. I'll go to surgical room A now."

Lead: "Yes Doctor." She gestures an orderly over. "Remove his clothes and drape him for surgery." Lead moves off to get supplies to start the IV. She returns and begins the procedure, finding a vein, applying the tourniquet, and then inserting the needle. The patient jerks awake as she does. She injects narcotics to ease him. But he grabs her hand, whispers. "Please."

Lead: "You are about to have surgery. Doctor will make you better."

Soldier: "Promise me."

Lead: "I promise you'll be better."

Soldier: "No. Promise." Voice trails off again as though he can't muster the energy to speak.

Lead: "Promise what?"

Soldier: "Promise me you won't let them..." his voice trails off again and he loses consciousness.

Lead gestures for the orderly to roll him into the surgical room. Lead moves over to help other QAs with the recent arrivals.

Scene Out

Scene In

Next day. Soldier is sitting up in bed. Half his right arm missing and bandaged and in a sling to keep it slightly elevated.

Lead comes through the ward checking on patients, taking vitals, joking with some, lighting cigarettes for others. She stops at his bed.

Lead: "Good morning. Good to see you up and about."

Soldier: "Bloody little up and about to it." Angry tone.

Lead: "No need to be dour. You'll be up striding about in no time."

Soldier: "Fat lot of good that will do me."

Lead: "So you lost your arm, many a soldier has given much more. And you'll learn to use your left hand in no time at all."

Soldier snorts: "I'm already left-handed."

Lead laughs uproariously and it rings through the tent, other soldiers joining in because they like to see her happy. After a moment the soldier in front of her chuckles weakly.

Soldier: "I suppose that is something to be grateful for. I won't have to learn to feed myself again."

Lead: "That's better. Now then I need to check your vitals and then I can light you a smoke."

The Soldier nodded. Lead begins the process, temperature, blood pressure, heart rate.

Lead: "How's your pain?"

Soldier: "I'll survive." Angry tone creeping back in.

Lead: "Can I light you a fag?"

Short nod by Soldier.

Lead does. "Want to tell me your name?"

Soldier: "Doesn't my file tell you all you need to know?" His tone should be angry and a touch snarky.

Lead: "I'd rather talk to you." Soft smile.

Soldier blinks. "Lieutenant Ian Tallsworth, but my friends call me Cooper."

Lead: "Nice to meet you, Lieutenant Tallsworth."

The soldier looks at her expectantly then shrugs.

Lead: "You can call me Sister." Then laughs.

She pats his leg and then moves onto the next patient. Tallsworth watches her move down the line of beds, joking and cajoling each one as needed.

Scene Out

My fingers were numb and my eyes burned with exhaustion. The plate of sandwiches held but a few crust ends and the coffee carafe was empty. My bladder was full and my brain in pain. I stumbled up the stairs to solve both of the latter problems. After attending to the former I peeled off my clothes as I stumbled to my bed, enjoying the pleasant thought, someone would clean them up first thing for me and I didn't need to check my bed for scorpions. The war was very close right now. I could almost smell the salt in the air as I drifted off to sleep.

CHAPTER NINE

WHERE I GIVE IN TO THE MUSE

I slept through early tea, breakfast, and late tea. When I awoke the sun was high in the sky, my clothes had been taken away for cleaning and in the magical way good servants have, mere moments after I sat up and stretched in bed, there was a gentle tap on the door and the upper house maid entered with hot coffee and toast.

"Good morning milady, a bit to get you by until cook gets lunch dished up."

I smiled. "Thank you, Mary."

I nibbled my toast, thickly spread with butter to the very edge of the crust. The coffee was strong and piping hot. I hoped the combination of the two would revive me. My brain still seemed to be asleep. I needed to write vastly more than I had last night. There was the rest of my time in Africa and then the trip home and my days in Europe to be covered. I wondered, if I gave up sleep for the rest of the weekend, could I be back at Rank with a completed script for Elizabeth Barrow by Monday? Then I laughed at myself. I couldn't get too caught up in the details. That was how you got overwhelmed. Best not to think of myself but to think of what I needed to do specifically. I pushed the covers back and gave myself a quick wash. I pulled my hair back into a very unfashionable bun. I slipped into crepe de chine pajamas and a matching robe and headed down to the library bypassing the dining room. Lunch could be served to me at my typewriter in my opinion.

Scene In:

The mess tent at night, cocktail hour. Lead is sipping a drink and reading a book at one of the tables. Another QA has invited Lt Tallsworth to the cocktail hour. He spies Lead and crosses to her, leaving his date behind.

Tallsworth: "Not socializing this evening?"

Lead: puts down her book with a smile. "I rarely socialize at these events."

Tallsworth: "I haven't seen you in my ward lately."

Lead: "I was moved out to the small pox quarantine tent."

Tallsworth: "Small pox? Isn't that dangerous?"

Lead: "I suppose so. I never much considered it but I suppose that's why they have trouble getting Sisters to work there."

Tallsworth: "You don't think about it?"

Lead: "Those men need help just like any other soldier." Matter of fact tone.

Tallsworth: "What's it like out there?"

Lead: "You almost found out yourself not that long ago." Said with a light laugh.

Tallsworth: Gestures to the second chair.

Lead nods.

Tallsworth: "What do you mean?" asks as he sits down.

Lead: "We had patients coming down with small pox in other tents."

Tallsworth: "I didn't hear about that."

Lead: "It was kept as quiet as it could be, of course. No one could figure it out. The Commander had the tent moved a mile from the rest of the hospital and still patients were popping up here."

Tallsworth: "Don't stop there, how did it all turn out?"

Lead: "Turned out ants were picking up the crusts that fell off the small pox blisters and carrying them through to the other tents."

Tallsworth: wrinkles his nose. "Nasty."

Lead: nods. "The quarantine tent has been moved five miles out now. Means a longer shift for those of us working out there but the infections have stopped spreading to the main hospital."

Silence for a moment while they both drink. Lead regards her drink, playing with the water ring on the table with her glass. Tallsworth regards her.

Lead: "You seem to be doing quite well these days."

Tallsworth: "Just waiting for a hospital ship back home."

Lead: "Are you being invalided out then?"

Tallsworth: "I'm no good to them anymore, not out here."

Lead: "I don't believe that. What was your job?"

Tallsworth: "RAF, spitfire."

Lead: "Oh." There wasn't much to be said to a pilot with one arm.

Another moment of silence, Tallsworth staring at his glass this time. A voice from across the room breaks the silence, the girl who invited Tallsworth calling him over.

Tallsworth: "I have to go back over to..." He gestures behind him rather than finishing the sentence and it should be obvious he doesn't want to name her. "I'll be catching that ship soon I think but I, I would like, is there any way-" He is interrupted by the appearance of his date.

Lead stands, pushing in her chair: "It was lovely to see you again Lt Tallsworth. Safe travels home."

Lead exits the tent as Tallsworth looks on and his date pulls at his good arm for his attention.

Scene Out

Quinten had delivered a plate of sandwiches while I typed up this scene and I stopped working to provide myself with some sustenance. But the ideas were flowing and I quickly began one-handed typing while I ate.

Scene In

In the grand ballroom of a great country estate, QAs standing in rows listening to the lecturing matron. "You must be constantly at the ready. You may not leave the estate. You may not mail any letters. You can collect twenty-four hours emergency rations as you leave this room. Keep them and the rest of your gear packed at all times. It will be very short notice to mobilize."

QAs file out picking up the little tin with rations. Our lead is among them. As she stops in the hall to open it a small group of QAs bunch up with her.

Lead: "Four cigarettes?"

New Friend: "It's the four pieces of lavatory paper that worry me." Laughing with a lilting Irish brogue.

Lead laughs with her. They move off together, separating from the group. Down the stairs, chatting as they go to the gardens outside.

New Friend: "Did I tell you about my trip out?"

Lead: "Not in detail."

New Friend: "So this one morn, we're all asleep in our racks when the alarm goes off. We leap out of beds, grab our floatie, and haul it up to the deck. I am sure the ship is going down and I don't swim a lick. As we stand there huddled together waiting for instructions we see seamen running about the ship. Then the Captain comes on over the speaker. The breakfast room has been smashed but if we are prepared to stand about deck for twenty minutes he'll have bacon and egg sammies served to us."

They both laugh.

Lead: "It could always be worse, did you hear about the QA who was too fat to get through the port hole and got stuck? The ship went down with her stuck there in the side."

New Friend: "Get away with you."

Lead: "No. I heard it from a good friend who was in 67th with me for a while."

New Friend: "She buy it?" asked in a matter of fact tone.

Lead: "No. She got posted after missing curfew out with a Yank." Said with a bit of a sigh and a wry smile.

New Friend: "Aye. I knew a few of those."

Lead: "It seems easier to just not socialize. No problems, no worries, no heartbreak."

New Friend: smiles as though she has a secret. "Sometimes it's worth the risk."

Lead: "I sense a story."

New Friend: "Nothing much to tell."

Lead: "Now why don't I believe that?"

New Friend: "It'll be something to tell if we both survive the war, alright then?"

Lead nods. "Alright then."

Camera watches them walk away.

Scene out

I moved through the day in a daze of the past and how to make it salable. Staff scurried out of my way as I moved past them in the hallways. I ignored everyone who tried to speak to me with a wave of my hand and a distant stare. I wrote until my fingers were aching and bloodied where I had broken three finger nails. I slept in the library that night, dozing fitfully and then waking to type off another scene or two.

CHAPTER TEN

WHERE I ENJOY AN INTERVENTION

The next afternoon found me unbathed and no longer bothering to eat, so tired of sandwiches, I couldn't bear another bite. Midafternoon the door of the library swung open loudly and Lila and Marlene swooped in with an apologetic Quinten not far behind.

"Darling, Quinten has been telling us you have Typhus or some such malarkey. But I'm quite worried about you. You missed our lunch date yesterday and not a word, a card, or flowers," Lila trilled.

"What day is it?" I asked vaguely confused. I hadn't remembered a lunch date.

"Sunday. Practically teatime." Lila sounded shocked. "We were supposed to have lunch and go look at the new hats yesterday."

Marlene removed her coat and hat and handed them to Quinten. In a low voice she gave him directions. "Please be so good as to have a house maid run a bath for her ladyship. Instruct the cook to prepare a meal to be served here when she is done."

Quinten nodded, likely pleased someone had come to put an end to the current state of insanity.

Marlene crossed to my desk. "Your maid is running your bath. I suggest you take advantage of it as a time to recharge your writing. I'll look over what you have so far while you do so."

"I can't waste time bathing."

Lila wrinkled her nose. "When was the last time you did? Or changed your clothes?"

I shook my head uncertain as to the answer to either. "It doesn't matter."

"Darling, you have something on what was once a very nice pair of crepe de chine pajammies and it smells a bit like fish." Lila leaned and sniffed hard.

I looked down and saw what she meant. I wrinkled my nose, then reached down to touch it. It was almost crumbly. How long had I been wearing these clothes? I stood and gathered my pages handing them off to Marlene as I made my way to the door. I stumbled upstairs and noticed the upper house maid watching me with concern from the landing.

"The water is warm for you, my lady."

I nodded. How much had I even written? I had lost the plot. The stack of pages seemed fairly thick. But I had no idea how many I needed. I submerged my body, then started scrubbing in earnest. The sooner I got done and back downstairs the faster I would know what Marlene had to say. Surely she could set me straight. I toweled off furiously fast and dashed to my wardrobe. Rummaging around I found some silk lounging trousers and a matching cashmere sweater. Wrapping my wet hair up in a turban, I dashed down the stairs breathless to hear what Marlene might say. I couldn't even entertain the notion she might tell me it was all balderdash. I popped through the door and practically shouted, "Well?"

Marlene looked up at me from over her reading glasses. "Sit and eat. Then we will talk."

An entire lunch had been laid out on the side table. Lila had already fixed herself a plate and was nibbling her way through foie gras and baked brie on toast points. At least there were no sandwiches in sight. I intended to only get a bite of something and sit down to wait impatiently, but as I filled my plate my stomach rumbled in anticipation and I found myself partaking of all the dishes and eating heartily.

Marlene finally put down my pages and removed her glasses. "You've really got something here."

My face broke into a grin. "I do." It was a statement, and the moment I heard her words I knew it to be true. The amount of pride that soared in my heart surprised me. I hadn't realized I had become attached to the project itself, not just as the solution to my Patrick problem.

"You need a bit more of course."

I nodded.

"And your formatting is enough to give me a migraine." Marlene sighed heavily.

"Formatting?"

"Yes. Scripts need to be in proper format. I'll rough out the basic idea for you so you can fix this mess." Marlene began to scribble on the page.

I nodded and waited to hear what she might say next.

"Alright, now where's the love interest?"

I shook my head with a start. "There isn't meant to be one. It's a story of the war, nurses' experiences in the war."

"Every script of this sort must have a love interest. Movies aren't made about women strictly for the sake of the woman. Give her a love interest."

Inwardly I groaned. I could write about Patrick I supposed, but that was taking this awfully close to the bone.

"Why not have her run into the pilot again," Marlene suggested.

I blinked. "What pilot?"

"The RAF she meets in Africa who has his arm amputated. He was clearly smitten with her."

"Oh him. No. No, he wasn't smitten with her. You're reading emotion that wasn't there."

"How do you know the emotion wasn't there? Did you know this young man in real life?"

"He was more an amalgamation of all the young pilots I met in the war."

Marlene spoke carefully, allowing her words to fall one at a time. "Be careful writing this so autobiographically."

"Why? You just said it was good."

Marlene took a deep breath. "When the story really happened to you, it lends an emotional connection that might make criticism difficult to accept."

"As long as Rank wants it, I don't much mind what they say." I dismissed her concerns.

Marlene paused as though considering the veracity of my statements. "As you please. I think when all is said and done once you add the love story, you have it."

That same huge goofy grin crossed my face. I was doing this. I would actually get a script into Rank and get to see Patrick.

"Darling, how many hidden talents you have." Lila smiled and drained her tea cup. "Shall we vacate and let you get back to your typewriting?"

I grinned. "Yes, please."

Lila stood and rang the bell for Quinten. When he came she smiled politely at him and then delivered one of her humorous little diatribes. "Quinten, you are an old and trusted servant here in the Leighton home. The state of Molly when we arrived was a disgrace. I charge you to ensure she eats, sleeps, and bathes daily."

Quinten nodded. "I shall do my best."

I laughed and crossed to my desk. "Goodbye dear Lila and thank you Marlene."

CHAPTER ELEVEN

WHERE I WRITE UNTIL IT HURTS

Quinten closed the library door behind my departing guests and I assumed they collected their coats and moved off into the big world outside my small sphere. But I was already lost again to the lore of the past. My fingers caressed the keys of my typewriter as I remembered. I could smell the hint of seaweed and oil. The sounds of machinery loud and purposeful, driving us forward in the darkness.

EXT TO INT. SHIP - NIGHT

The QAs have been mobilized and are boarding a ship. All lights are out. Our lead and her new friend stick together.

NEW FRIEND

I hope we don't get sunk.

LEAD

You really should have learned to swim but I'll get you across if it comes to that.

MONTAGE

1. Night crossing. Very black.

2. They land on a series of docks floating quite a way into the channel as the beaches are all torn up.

3. The women hurry into the back of covered trucks, which take them to their hospitals.

4. They sit on boards along the sides, shown before the back truck flaps are rolled down closing them into the dark.

5. As Lead and New Friend exit their truck, jumping down into mud, the matron is waiting for them.

MATRON

Welcome to Harley Street Ladies.

NEW FRIEND

(said with a quipping tone of voice)

I knew that ship took a wrong turn somewhere.

MATRON

(smiles briefly in acknowledgment to this bit of humor then is all business.)

This close to the front line, you experience a lot of freedom. Doctors are busy with the dying. Everyone else will be at your discretion. You diagnose, you treat, you send 'em back.

LEAD

(asked with a raised eyebrow and half a smile.)

So the status quo is official here?

The matron laughs. Lead and New friend join in.

EXT. COUNTRYSIDE - DAY

New friend and Lead, in off hours, in a tree copse, drinking champagne from the bottle and trading stories.

LEAD

Where were you before?

NEW FRIEND

Before this glorious posting? (She waves her arm around and laughs, a little drunk already.)

I was in India for eighteen months.

LEAD

Tell me all about India.

NEW FRIEND

India was strange. I was in a base hospital and the patients were airlifted in from Burma. For every injured man, we got a hundred with Malaria.

LEAD

Get out!

NEW FRIEND

No really. I heard the annual malaria rate was above eighty percent of the total strength of the army.

LEAD

I can't imagine it.

NEW FRIEND

Anyway, that's how I ended up back in England. Malaria.

LEAD

You got sick?

NEW FRIEND

I did. They insisted we wear our traditional uniform. The mosquitoes just ate our bare legs alive.

LEAD

I had it fairly easy in Africa but I heard stories from other sisters on the ship on our way back to England.

NEW FRIEND

Entertain me.

LEAD

This one nurse told me she got the idea to put her bed legs in tins of kerosene so the scorpions that tried to climb into her bed would drown on their way up.

NEW FRIEND

Did it work?

LEAD

I guess so. She never got bit while she was out there.

Both girls laugh.

LEAD

She also told me this story about her tent mate who got all prepared to take a proper bath only to discover when she was done she had forgotten to close the outer flaps on her tent and every soldier in the yard …

NEW FRIEND

(gasps)

Not so.

LEAD

Indeed. Would I lie?

NEW FRIEND (in sync verbally with Lead)

Rarely.

More laughter.

INT. HOSPITAL TENT - DAY

There is a rush of new patients. The Lead begins tending to a young man with cool grey eyes and sandy blond hair. He is burned on his back. She squats to the side of his bed.

PATIENT

How bad is it?

LEAD

You've got a bit of a burn. I'll treat it for you and you'll be right as rain.

PATIENT

Will it hurt?

LEAD

A brave soldier like you can handle a bit of a pain, I'm sure.

LEAD begins picking out the debris from his wound. She grinds up sulfonamide and sprinkles it into the wound to prevent septicemia. She then covers the wound with clean bandaging.

INT HOSPITAL TENT - EARLY MORNING

It is implied it is the next morning. The LEAD is making her rounds. She squats down next to the PATIENT with the burned back from the day before.

> LEAD
>
> How are you feeling this morning?
>
> PATIENT
>
> (smiles at Lead)
>
> Better now that I see you.
>
> LEAD
>
> (returns smile)

I need to check your wound. Are you ready for that?

PATIENT nods.

LEAD removes bandage, sprinkles in more powder. Pokes at a few places to see if pus comes out.

> LEAD
>
> It is looking fairly good all things considered.
>
> PATIENT
>
> You wouldn't lie to a soldier now would you?

LEAD

(with a laugh)

Rarely.

PATIENT

Have you heard what happened to rest of my unit?

LEAD

(With shake of her head.)

Were you all injured?

PATIENT

A bomb dropped on our position. The roof caved in. I tried to pull out as many as I could but the fire was so intense I just couldn't see.

LEAD

(Places her hand on his shoulder.)

I can't imagine how terrifying it must be to lose your friends like that.

PATIENT

I only wish I could have done more.

LEAD smiles at PATIENT who returns her smile.

MONTAGE - LOVE GROWS BETWEEN LEAD AND PATIENT

1. Many scenes of the two of them talking.

2. Lead stops by far more often than she needs to, stopping at his bed on the way up and down the tent, every time.

3. Lots of laughter shots.

4. LEAD touches PATIENT on hand or arm frequently.

INT. NURSES TENT - NIGHT - LIT BY LANTERN HANGING BETWEEN CAMP BEDS

> NEW FRIEND
>
> I haven't seen you much these last few days.
>
> LEAD
>
> I've been busy on the wards.
>
> NEW FRIEND
>
> On the wards or with that pretty soldier?
>
> LEAD
>
> Whichever soldier do you mean?
>
> NEW FRIEND
>
> You know who I mean. The one with the burned back. Good thing it left his pretty face untouched, aye?

LEAD

(With laughter)

Patrick Dumont.

I stopped mid scene. I couldn't call him by his real name. When Rank got the script it would be a disaster. I rolled out the page, retyped the portion until I needed to name him, then started again.

LEAD

(With laughter.)

Reginald Travers.

NEW FRIEND

That's the one.

LEAD sighs.

NEW FRIEND

(With a mildly haughty tone, gently mocking Lead.)

And here I thought you didn't believe in socializing with the soldiers, it was not worth the risk.

LEAD

(With hearty laughter.)

Did I ever say that? I must have been crazy.

> NEW FRIEND
>
> (laughs with Lead.)
>
> Must have been.

INT. HOSPITAL TENT - NIGHT

On the ward, after lights out, Lead sneaks in a bottle of champagne.

> LEAD
>
> (Whispering close to PATIENT'S ear)
>
> Are you awake?
>
> PATIENT
>
> (Smiles and then opens his eyes.)
>
> Always for you.
>
> LEAD
>
> I brought you some champagne.
>
> PATIENT
>
> Champagne? How did you manage that?
>
> LEAD
>
> It's easier to get champagne right now than it is to get water. At least for officers.

PATIENT

I noticed your two pips.

LEAD

(With a glance at her uniform.)

It's standard operating procedure.

PATIENT

Do they give you a hard time because I'm not?

LEAD

(Playful tone.)

Not what?

PATIENT

An officer.

LEAD

I haven't much asked anyone's opinion.

PATIENT

But your commander must have an opinion she can share as she pleases.

LEAD

The matron you mean? I don't think she's noticed. You've only been here a few days.

PATIENT

We'll have to be careful then.

LEAD leans in to kiss patient. Don't actually show the kiss.

INT. HOSPITAL TENT - DAY

Lead stands at empty bed for a moment then turns in a panic to the nearest patient.

LEAD

Where is he?

OTHER PATIENT

Moved out first thing this morning. Hospital ship back to jolly old England.

LEAD

(Runs to the ward nurse.)

The patient, with the back burn, he was transferred this morning?

WARD NURSE

(With an earnest and haughty tone.)

He was and if you ask me it was a good thing too.

LEAD

Well I didn't ask you.

WARD NURSE

We are supposed to be an example of unselfishness, self-sacrifice, and indefatigable devotion to duty, not love struck little idiots looking for a husband.

Lead's face tightens but she bites her tongue and stomps off.

EXT FIELD BETWEEN TENTS - DAY

LEAD

(With a morose tone.)

He's gone.

NEW FRIEND

(In confusion and shock.)

Who? Wait, your soldier? He died?

LEAD

(Scoffs.)

Bite your tongue. No, he got transferred to a hospital ship this morning.

NEW FRIEND

So you'll write, he'll write, and after the war-

LEAD begins to cry.

NEW FRIEND

You didn't exchange addresses?

LEAD shakes head.

NEW FRIEND

But you know his last name?

LEAD

Of course I know that but not much else. He grew up in the country but hasn't lived there in years.

NEW FRIEND

I have faith, if you are meant to be together, you will be able to find him after the war.

LEAD

(With a small smile and a sniff.)

You have faith?

NEW FRIEND

They say I'm a little touched by the fairies. I see a future with this man.

LEAD

(Big smile now, dries her tears.)

I believe you.

NEW FRIEND

(With a laugh.)

Double wedding when we all get back from over here.

LEAD

(Sticks out her hand and they shake on it.)

Absolutely.

I had to stop writing for the night. All the reminders of Frankie and what she meant to me were open weeping wounds. I knew what needed to come next but I couldn't do it now. It would have to wait for morning, when I was fresh.

CHAPTER TWELVE

WHERE I LOSE EVERYTHING ELSE

When I awoke the next day I did not rush down to my desk and begin typing furiously as I had done in previous days. Instead, I drank my coffee in bed before heading down to the dining room to eat breakfast in leisure. After I had my third, procrastinating cup of coffee, I finally headed to the library but still I did not type. I returned my father's phone call from days earlier.

"Goodwin Estate, how many I assist you?" Wadsworth's cultured voice slipped through the phone line in mellow tones.

"Good morning Wadsworth. May I speak to my father?"

"His lordship is with the architect at this time. Would you like me to interrupt him?"

I pondered this briefly, interrupt my father and have a less than pleasant conversation with him or tackle writing about one of the hardest days of my life. No contest. "Please do. I'll hold."

It was some minutes before I heard my father. "So you've finally deigned to return my call."

"Good morning to you too Father." I kept my voice light and cheerful.

"You seem in spirits. You haven't been imbibing them have you?"

I gave him a courtesy laugh. "No, Father. I have simply found something to do with my time that thrills me."

"When you describe it like that, it worries me."

"I am writing. It is a noble calling as you will agree I am sure."

There was a long pause. So long in fact I was concerned we had been disconnected and I would have to start the whole process over.

"Are you still there or have we been disconnected?"

"Margaret I am speechless. Good for you."

"Thank you."

"I'll let your mother know you won't be coming home in the immediate future and she will have to wait until the hunting party weekend to see you."

I gasped. I had completely forgotten to handle the hunting party situation with my mother.

"You will be coming home for that. Your mother is expending a lot of effort to arrange a delightful weekend." His tone brooked no dissent.

I whispered, "Yes, Father."

"Very good. Let me know when you are done with your literary effort and I will find you a publisher."

"Thank you Father," I whispered even more weakly. I would have to explain about the film script some other time. The reminder of the husband hunting party was more than I could tackle in one morning as it was.

"Til then."

"Yes, til then." I rang off straight away before he could say anything else that might do my heart damage. I couldn't possibly write about Frankie in this state. I would skip ahead and invent a scene where our leading lady returns to England after the war. Her soldier is waiting for her at the dock having found out ahead of time when her hospital was dismantled and she was sent back home. Their romantic reunion and subsequent marriage would make a lovely ending to this tale of the heartbreak of war.

It took me the better part of the morning to handle the scene to my satisfaction. I broke for a proper lunch and then made more calls. My first call was to Elizabeth Barrow. She was much easier to get on the phone than Patrick, apparently girls weren't queuing for her attentions.

"I have the script almost done. I should be able to run it out to you this afternoon."

"Remind me again who you are?"

I paused. "Molly Leighton. We met when I auditioned as an actress and I had no experience." When Elizabeth didn't respond I continued, "We talked on the way out and you said you were looking for scripts. I offered you one and you said you would look at it?"

"Oh, oh, yes. Right. You don't need to bring it by yourself. Just have it messengered over to my attention."

"I'll do that."

"Thanks for calling. Ta."

She rang off before I could say anything more. I sat looking at the phone in my hand for a moment. That had been less than reassuring. Eventually the beeping from the phone stopped and the operator asked if I needed assistance to dial a call. Startled I snapped out a no and then hung up the receiver, annoyed with myself for wool gathering when there was work to be done.

I rolled a clean sheet of paper into the typewriter and adjusted the alignment. With a deep sigh I rested my fingers on the keys and my palm on the hand rest. The words didn't want to come. Clearly I needed assistance. I rang the bell and ordered a Sidecar when Alice arrived to answer it. I waited impatiently for her to bring me the drink and gulped it off in one draught.

EXT. DIRT ROAD SOME SHRUBBERY JEEP DRIVING AWAY IN THE BACKGROUND - DAY

Lead and her New Friend walking back along Caen Bayeux road having just declined a ride in a jeep with two soldiers.

NEW FRIEND

Would it really have been so bad if we let them drive us back?

LEAD

We would have been leading them on.

NEW FRIEND

How do you figure that?

LEAD

Both our hearts belong to others.

NEW FRIEND

I doubt they wanted our hands in marriage, more likely our easy wit and lovely visage for company.

LEAD

(With a laugh.)

You're right. I'm being an idiot. Next time we can take the ride.

NEW FRIEND

Good to know you still see reason under all that romantic malarkey.

Both women laugh and continue to walk. Not much further down the road a plane is heard overhead. They emerge from the trees into a field area of the road, as they do an unexpected Luftwaffe plane strafes the road. New Friend is hit. Lead dives into a gully and escapes uninjured. She rushes to New Friend and tries to stop the bleeding but New Friend dies within minutes. Lead cries heartily for a few minutes.

LEAD

So much for our double wedding then.

Lead pulls New Friend's body up and over her shoulder and begins walking back to camp carrying her dead body. Arms should hang down her back moving as she bears the heavy burden.

I cried for quite some time when I finished writing the scene. Then I rang the bell and ordered another Sidecar. Alice eyed me carefully but brought me the drink anyway. What did I care if she thought two cocktails before three in the afternoon was scandalous.

CHAPTER THIRTEEN

WHERE I HANDLE MY BUSINESS

When I finished my second drink I bundled up the script and placed it in a large manila envelope with a quick note to Elizabeth Barrow. I addressed the envelope and instructed Quinten to arrange for a messenger to pick up the package and deliver it immediately. Then I went upstairs to sleep off the emotional fog.

Tuesday morning I awoke full of anticipation. I bathed carefully and made sure my favorite suit was perfectly pressed. I wanted to be impeccable when I went to the studio to negotiate my position. I planned to insist on Patrick in the male lead role and a position for myself as some sort of on the set daily type of role. I didn't even know what that might be. I decided to call Lila for Marlene's exchange number.

"Marlene, Molly Leighton here."

"Ah, yes, how is your opus coming along?"

"I sent it off to be read, I expect to hear back any time now."

Marlene coughed, or perhaps she laughed and turned it into a cough to be kind. "When did you turn it in?"

"I had it messengered over yesterday."

"Did your contact tell you to expect to hear something today?" Marlene asked in a kind voice as though she was talking to a small child.

"Well no but surely-"

"Molly, my dear you have a lot to learn about this business. It might be months before you hear a word from Rank."

My stomach plummeted, "Months?" I almost wailed.

"Yes. Months, if ever."

Her matter of fact tone made me want to cry. "But you said it was good."

"It was good, but that means very little in the film world. No matter how good your script is, if no one wants to produce it, you are out of luck."

"Produce it?" I was so confused, my disappointment was making my brain process slowly.

Marlene sighed. "The producer is *the* man. The man with the juice. He makes things happen. Gets people hired or fired, and he gets the money to make the film."

"I thought that was the director," I mewed plaintively.

"A director picks the script, gets approval from the producer, then takes the script and tells the actors how to act."

"Oh." I felt slightly at a loss. "So if I was planning to ask for a position on the film, what should I say?"

"You want to be in on the making of this film?" Marlene sounded surprised.

"I do."

"I thought you just wanted to see that little soldier boy of yours."

"I do, but I need time on the lot to find him." I paused. I wanted her opinion on what I was considering saying next but I was also afraid to hear what she might say. If she panned my idea I might be afraid to say it to the studio. With a deep breath I blurted it out, "I was thinking of asking they make him the male lead in the film."

"They might be willing, if they want your script bad enough."

"And then what job do I ask for?"

"You'll have to beg and be exceedingly lucky but you might ask to assist the director."

"Assistant director?"

Marlene laughed. "No. That is something entirely different. When you assist the director you are in a learning position. You'll end up fetching his coffee and giving people messages from him, taking messages for him, menial work but you would be on the set daily and then some."

"I could do that." I felt reassured by her answer. I had been moving forward on sheer luck and hard work so far. I saw no reason why it shouldn't get me where I needed to go this time.

"I wish you good luck Molly; I think you are going to need it." Her voice was doubtful.

I felt on more solid footing. I was grateful that Marlene provided a dose of reality throughout this project. "Thank you again Marlene."

With potentially months to wait, I debated what to do with myself. I couldn't go to the country house unless I wanted to discuss plans for the upcoming husband hunting party and be queried at length by my father about my novel. London was emptying out of people going abroad for the winter or to their country estates to shoot, before going abroad for the winter. Lila suggested we could go away for a bit but I wanted to stay close to the phone.

Monday, the week after I turned in my script, I called Elizabeth Barrow. She was unavailable this time but I left a message. I called Tuesday as well, another message. And Wednesday. And Thursday. And Friday. When this produced no results, I started the following week by heading to the Rank lot in Islington first thing Monday morning.

CHAPTER FOURTEEN

WHERE I GO TO THE LOT, AGAIN

The gargoyle was in attendance at her desk when I arrived. I smiled my brightest smile and asked ever so politely to see Elizabeth Barrow.

"Who should I say is here?"

"Lady Margaret Leighton."

The gargoyle's eyes narrowed. "Haven't you been here before?"

"I have."

"What did I tell you about impersonating the nobility?"

I sighed. "As I told you before I am Lady Margaret Leighton and I would like to see Elizabeth Barrow."

The gargoyle stared at me for a long moment. "I'll call her."

"Thank you." I tried to keep my feeling of glee at this minor victory out of my tone of voice.

She dialed the phone and must have gotten through to someone. I listened to her end of the conversation. "For Elizabeth, Lady Leighton is here." Pause. "I'll tell her." She hung up. "Elizabeth is too busy to see you today."

I smiled. "I'll wait." Then I walked over and sat in one of the thoughtfully provided chairs. I opened my bag and took out a copy of Jane Austen's *Persuasion*. It wasn't my favorite Austen but I hoped the title might give the gargoyle ideas.

The gargoyle snorted and continued her work. After some time when she saw I meant to stay as long as it took, she picked up her phone and dialed out again. "Lady Leighton is willing to wait, all day it appears, to see Elizabeth." There was a pause as she listened. "I see." She hung up and smiled at me; an honest to God real smile.

"Elizabeth will be here to collect you shortly."

I may have imagined it but I thought I detected a hint of pleasant surprise in her tone. I smiled in return and put my book away. Slipping out a compact I checked my lipstick and reassured myself my nose did not need powdering. Minutes slipped by but I was content to wait. Finally the inner door banged open and Elizabeth rushed out. "Well come on you, I don't have all day."

I followed her with all appearance of meekness and a gentle smile on my face but one knows what the good book says about the meek. My wants were tamer than the whole earth but I intended to inherit none the less. I followed Elizabeth out of the administration building and into a smaller building with offices and conference rooms.

It was into one of the latter that she directed me, while barking for someone to bring us coffee.

"Yes, I got your script. Yes, I read your script. Yes, I showed your script to the director."

I smiled.

"Don't get too eager. He says war stories have been done. He won't make another."

I deflated on the spot. I would inherit nothing.

"However, he does like your main character and some of the supporting roles you have written into the script. He would like to see you write a love story involving this character without the war."

I swallowed hard. "I -"

Elizabeth held up her hand as coffee was brought in. She waited until the underling had exited and closed the door behind him. "He also would like to see the new script in a similar timeline as the last one."

I choked on the air I was gasping in. "How fast does he want it?"

Elizabeth smiled. "One week."

"I can't do that," I blurted in desperation. I had forgotten about arguing that I didn't have anything else to write about. At this point I was struck by the stark impossibility of writing anything I hadn't lived through, in a week.

"I could coax him into ten days," Elizabeth offered in seriousness, as though three extra days would make all the difference.

"That's still, barely any time at all, and I have to spend the weekend at my parents' country estate shooting."

Despair dripped from my voice but Elizabeth bristled at the mention of my weekend plans.

"Look, this is it. Your one chance. Take it or don't. But don't sit there sniveling to me about the hardships of being rich and titled." Her tone was hard.

I nodded. "Of course, my apologies."

"So I can tell Coop you'll have something for us late next week?"

I nodded faintly, unable to speak.

"Good." Elizabeth stood and stuck out her hand at the same time. I weakly shook it. "I look forward to hearing from you."

She left the room and stalked off. I found my way off the film lot in a daze, only realizing as I was blocks away down the street, that I had just frittered away the perfect chance to locate Patrick. I could have searched for him right then. I stopped hard in my tracks. There was nothing for it; I would simply have to write the new script.

CHAPTER FIFTEEN

WHERE I RUSH AROUND LIKE A CHICKEN WITH MY HEAD CUT OFF

I hurried back to the Grosvenor Square house to pack my belongings. If I had to go to the country this weekend, I might as well go today. I could ponder topics and plots on the train and then write undisturbed until the potential suitors descended in three days. Why hadn't I just told my mother no in the first place? As I flew through the front door I tossed my gloves on the side table and asked Quinten to order me a taxi for the train, I was going back to Goodwin.

"Yes, milady, and I'll send Mary up to you to pack."

I didn't bother to argue this time. That was fine by me. I needed to put together a bag so I could work on the train, long hand as it were. When Mary entered the room I gestured at my wardrobe. "Hunting party weekend with lots of eligible bachelors my mother wants to marry me off to. Pack as you see fit. I need to attend to other things."

"Yes, my lady," She sounded distinctly relieved.

I hurried back downstairs. I hoped there was a typewriter at Goodwin. Surely my father must have one in his office. If not, I could write it all longhand and type it up when I returned to London on Monday. I was eager to be off and by that vein get started on this new script. I dabbled with the idea that I might even be a little excited about the script for the sake of the script. It surprised me to think perhaps I was a budding writer after all, not just a little love sick idiot.

Once I was safely ensconced on the train I turned honestly to solving the issue of a new plot. It was flattering to hear they liked me as a character but I didn't have a love story to tell that didn't involve the war. I had never been in love except for Patrick and that love story was wrapped up in the war. There would be no further chapters to that tale unless I could write this script however. Somewhere around Basingstoke I realized I already had the solution. I could write a script about this effort I was making to see Patrick again. Write a script about an ex QA who tries to be reunited with her soldier after the war. She sees him on a film poster. Tracks down the film studio he is under contract to. Auditions as an actress. And finally writes a film script that stars him, they fall madly in love and live happily ever after. I would have to actually fictionalize a lot but I already had hopes of how this would all turn out. Why not turn those hopes into a concrete way to make my dreams come true?

As the train pulled into Portsmouth I had already jotted down a number of little sketches and scenes to start to create a script but further work would have to wait until I successfully parried with my father and mother about my early arrival and could retire to a quiet sitting room as far out of the way of the main house as I could get.

Thoughtful Quinten had called ahead to Goodwin and notified Wadsworth of my arrival. Wadsworth in turn had sent Charles with the car. In no time at all I was sailing through the countryside in the back of my favorite Rolls Royce Silver Wraith. I tried to rehearse what I would say to my father. But these things never go as planned.

Wadsworth directed me to the race track site when I inquired of my father. I decided to tackle him later. "Could you provide me with a typewriter Wadsworth and set it up in…" I paused. "Which sitting room or morning room or lounge," I whirled my hand in the air to imply I didn't much care what sort of room it was, "is the least used at this time of year?"

Wadsworth considered, "The dowager's morning room in the East wing is quite unused due to the damp. However, I could have a fire built there for you and I think you could be tolerably comfortable and very much undisturbed."

"Perfect. You always know."

"Her ladyship has heard of your expected early arrival and wanted to see you upon your entrance."

I sighed. I also appreciated Wadsworth's subtle suggestion that I had not arrived home unless I chose to announce I had and told him so. "It must be done I suppose if I am to have any peace."

"She's in her sun room."

I nodded my thanks, although I was feeling less thankful by the moment, and headed off to beard the lioness in her den. I paused at the closed door to verify my stockings were straight, my hem was even, my nose powdered and my lipstick fresh. One always needed the appropriate armor for the battle at hand.

CHAPTER SIXTEEN

WHERE I AM DEFEATED BY A VACUOUS SINGLE-MINDED FOE

My mother was behind her desk writing letters. She slid the one she was working on under her blotter in response to my greeting. "Hello Margaret my dear. You are home early. Excited about the weekend?"

I smiled. "Mother, it's time for complete honesty. I do not want to get married."

"Nonsense darling, every woman wants to get married." My mother dismissed my opinion without further thought.

Oh to be that secure in your belief system. "I do not. I am writing. I want to be a writer."

"Do you really think it's wise to get too involved in those intellectual pursuits? Some men would balk at such a wife."

I sighed. "I will say this very slowly and with words of one syllable. I. Do. Not. Want. To. Get. Mar. Ried."

"I believe you will find married is really two syllables darling. A writer would know such things."

My hands formed into fists and I took a deep breath desperate not to lose my temper. My mother's calm and dispassionate tone was galling to no end.

"On Thursday evening five of the most eligible bachelors of the realm and three slightly less desirable but still acceptable bachelors will arrive. They will be here until Sunday teatime. You will behave in a manner befitting your upbringing. What you do between now and then is your business. If you wish to write," she made it sound like I was planning to breed black beetles, "then so be it."

I summoned a smile from the far depths of my soul and thanked her verbally while mentally adding thanks for my escape from this room right now. I hurried to the far side of the house where the dowager's morning room usually lay dormant. There had not been a dowager in residence in quite some time. Wadsworth had provided a roaring fire, black coffee in a carafe, and cookies, fruit, and nuts on a tray. Somewhere, I knew better than to ask where, he had procured a brand new IBM electric typewriter. I had heard tale that some very qualified typists could get upwards of ninety words a minute on these newfangled machines. I was thrilled to try it out.

I wrote all day, telling the part of the tale I already knew. Once an hour I broke to take a brisk walk up and down the corridor outside my morning room. This part of the house was oldest and always coldest, so the brisk air added to my efficiency when I went back to the table to work. Wadsworth alerted me when dinner would be ready in thirty minutes with his suggestion I had just time to dress. I declined and continued to type. At five minutes to seven the door opened and someone stood there until I stopped typing and turned to find my father.

"While I appreciate your endeavors, while you stay here, you will join us for dinner, you will dress for the occasion. You have four minutes. I suggest you hurry."

I knew better than to argue with my father when he employed that tone of voice. Instead I switched off the power to my new mechanical friend. My father had left after delivering his law. Three minutes to run across the house, upstairs, into a fancy dress and back down to the dining room. Hopeless. I would be late. Might as well take my time. My finger meandered toward the power button under its own volition, maybe I could write just a few more lines. Beatrice appeared in the door with my black velvet marocain. "Quickly my lady, you have no time to lose." I grinned at Wadsworth's ingenuity as I unbuttoned and slipped out of my shirt waist dress. It pooled to the floor at my feet as Beatrice slipped the new gown over my head. I kicked my day dress away as I wrestled with my zipper. Beatrice moved on to my hair and pulled it into a quick twist, sticking pins in as I was already heading for the door.

"Your shoes!" Beatrice exclaimed.

I kicked off the ones I was wearing as she handed me kitten heels. I started down the hall at breakneck speed and slipped into my heels as I arrived at the door to the dining room. I took a deep breath to calm myself, then plastered a serene smile on my face as I pushed back the door.

CHAPTER SEVENTEEN

WHERE I FEEL LIKE THE MAIN COURSE, SERVED FOR THE EVENING MEAL

I was just a moment late as I slid into my chair. My brothers and parents already seated. My oldest brother's wife came in a moment after me, but all was forgiven for her, given her very advanced state.

My father gave me a long look but I smiled pleasantly at him. I was not about to rat out the good Wadsworth or the good at following his orders Beatrice.

My oldest brother was distracted fussing over his wife. But my youngest brother, who has always been something of an imp, and therefore one of my favorite playmates when we were both home on holiday, was fully prepared to make trouble. "Molly, Father was just telling us all during cocktails that you are writing a novel." I recognized his tone as the one he employed when pretending to be innocent.

I smiled.

Nicholas continued on, "I find that very hard to believe."

My father interjected, "I actually observed Margaret in the process of writing mere minutes ago." He stressed my full name, the nickname of Molly irritated him as always. Nicholas was the only one who used the abbreviation in front of my father and while they never actually fought over it, the subtext contained a never ending argument.

Nicholas raised an eyebrow at me. "Tell the truth Molly, are you really writing the next great piece of heavily complicated British literature?"

I swallowed and smiled weakly. Nicholas and I had a deal, forged when we were eight and nine, respectively, and our older brother Stephen had played a long running joke on the two of us regarding the health of a much loved springer spaniel, Tiffy. He convinced us she had cancer and the tumor was growing exponentially. Finally when she disappeared for two days he convinced us she had run off to die alone. We were inconsolable until the stable hand announced Tiffy had whelped six wriggly puppies. We made this deal on the spot. Two deals actually. The first was that we would hate Stephen forever more and never ever speak to him again. The more important deal was that if one of us asked the other to 'tell the truth' we would instantly cease whatever game or trick we were playing and fess up.

"It's not actually a novel I am writing." I tried to speak in the lowest tone of voice I could possibly use and still maintain the illusion of good manners.

Instant silence attended the table. Forks were lowered to plates. Glasses were set down with their contents untasted. I smiled wanly and hoped I wouldn't actually be sick at the dinner table. "It's a screen play." I decided to employ Nicholas's innocent tone of voice.

My father's face became an instant scowl of disapproval. "What a ridiculous waste of time. Do you expect someone to make a movie from this screen play?"

"I do actually."

"Out of the question. I won't help you make any connections."

"I already have a studio and director interested, Rank Films."

"And how did you manage that?" My father snarled in disbelief.

I was considering how to finesse the situation without exposing myself to further ridicule when Nicholas chimed in, "I think I remember Lila having some film connections."

I stared at Nicholas. How did he know that?

"Lila who?" My father snapped.

"Lila O'Rourke," Nicholas answered.

"Who is that?" My father's anger was only growing with each passing question.

My mother stirred from her end of the table. "You remember dear, she was at Stonecroft with Margaret."

"That dreadful girl whose father made his millions in iron and thought that should give him access to a higher sphere than he deserved." My father was practically foaming at the mouth.

I nodded silently. There was no way I was going to get out of this dinner without giving my father a pound of flesh. I took a long drink of wine and braced myself for the diatribe to come.

Stephen stopped murmuring to his wife and addressed the table in a loud voice that would eventually carry well in the House of Lords. "All this arguing is upsetting Meredith. Stop being petty and do think of her delicate health. You can argue later."

I heard Nicholas choke back a snort or perhaps it was going to be a laugh. I bit the inside of my cheek to remain straight faced. My father stared long and hard at my eldest brother, then swallowed a sip of wine before he apologized for disturbing Meredith. In her timid voice she demurred.

The table was silent for several minutes as we all regrouped. This apparently gave Nicholas plenty of time to think of some new devilment.

"I hear half the heirs for the House of Lords will be in attendance this weekend."

My mother rose to the bait she did not perceive, and smiled as she replied, "I am quite pleased with the potential turnout."

Nicholas threw a glance my way. "Is Molly?"

"Is Margaret what? Speak in full sentences please Nicholas." My mother set her wine glass down heavily in her exasperation.

"Is Molly pleased with the potential turn out? After all it is her marriage market, is it not?"

My father cleared his throat but did enter the fray this time.

My mother gave Nicholas a long, slightly confused look. "How could Margaret not be pleased? Every woman wants to make an advantageous marriage. Meredith agrees with me, right dear?"

Meredith nodded and smiled sweetly.

I sighed. Did I want to launch another battle at the table? I did not. I took a sip of my soup and remained mum.

Nicholas turned to me and pointedly asked, "Do you want to make an advantageous marriage, Molly?"

I swallowed my soup and tried not to choke. I glanced at my father; he narrowed his eyes at me. I glanced at my mother who raised an eyebrow at me. "Someday," I responded hopefully.

Nicholas wrinkled his nose at me and I knew he was thinking I was a chicken. Before he could ask me to tell him the truth I asked my father in a rush how the plans for the race track were coming.

He had clearly been waiting for someone to ask or perhaps he wanted to avoid any more dangerous topics in deference to Meredith's delicate condition, because he spoke at length about the designs and about the designer in fulsome praise. I wondered again if he was entertaining the idea of marrying me off to his architect.

By the time he finished we were into the cheese course. Perhaps it was our full bellies, or perhaps we were all lulled into a half sleeping state by the long lecture on the intricacies of motor race courses, but the conversation was mundane for the rest of the meal. When my mother and Meredith stood to leave the dining room my father requested I remain behind. How silly of me to think I might actually escape without further ado.

CHAPTER EIGHTEEN

WHERE I HAVE TO GIVE AN ADDITIONAL POUND OF FLESH

I sat on the edge of my chair, literally and figuratively, while Wadsworth poured the men glasses of port and lit their cigars. My father leaned back in his chair, port in one hand and cigar in the other. "I want to discuss with you the seriousness of the situation you seem to have gotten yourself into."

I put on my most attentive face.

"For someone of our position to become involved with the film industry is a disgrace."

Stephen opened his fatuous mouth, "Did you even consider how your actions would reflect on the family name?"

"Honestly, no. The family name was not on my mind." Stephen's unneeded interference provoked me into speaking where I had planned to take my lashings in silence in the hope it would end all the sooner.

"Of course not. It's bad enough you had to go off and join the QAs rather than staying at home raising funds and knitting as a proper lady would have done."

I turned on Stephen angry at his presumption. "Like Meredith did you mean? And I deny your assumed right to tell me what to do."

"How dare you denigrate my wife?" Stephen stood and threw his napkin down on the table. If I had been a man he would have challenged me to step outside with him, I am certain. I would have respected him more if he had challenged me.

Nicholas interjected on my behalf, "She didn't. Following the logical train of thought she confirmed your belief that your wife is your ideal of how a lady should behave."

Stephen glared at Nicholas. Nicholas had always been smarter and quicker of wit. It infuriated Stephen from the moment their tutor had made it clear back when they were boys in the school room.

My father interrupted their battle before it could get ugly, "Enough."

Stephen lowered his glare and his bottom, then returned his focus to his cigar and port. Nicholas raised an eyebrow at me but did not challenge my father further, yet.

"Margaret, look at what your behavior is doing to our family and you haven't even finished this script."

"I don't see that my writing a script is doing anything to the family, Father. Your reactions to what you perceive might happen after I write the script is what is causing all this fuss."

"Do not play word games with me young lady. I will not have a daughter of mine selling herself."

I gasped at the inference. I ground my teeth together in an effort to keep my tone such that my father would perceive it as respectful. "I am not selling myself. I am creating a product which I am selling."

We glared at each other for a long moment. Nicholas began to hum Beethoven's fifth with dramatic flair.

"I begin to come round to your mother's way of thinking. You should get married as soon as possible. Then you will be someone else's problem to keep proper."

This was drastic means and required a drastic reply. "What if I used another name? A pseudonym?"

Stephen chimed in again, "Fat lot of good that will do when you pop out of a car at the premier."

"I won't be doing that." Couldn't the ignorant git keep his mouth closed.

My father queried, "You will not?"

"No. I don't want to be some ridiculous spectacle. I just want to make a movie, quietly."

"You will not use your proper name then?"

"No. I'll use Molly and," I looked frantically around the room for inspiration, "Wadsworth. Or just Worth." Wadsworth almost smiled; I could see the crinkle at the edge of his eyes.

Stephen sat steaming. "You can't really be considering this can you father?"

My father gave him another long look. I felt a moment of pity for Stephen. It must be hard sometimes to be the heir apparent. Perhaps my father sensed Nicholas was about to start humming again because he quickly made a 'this is over gesture,' sliding his hands parallel to the table in opposite directions. "Margaret, you may write your script if you use a pseudonym."

"But father-"

"Enough Stephen. The situation barely concerns you. The family name will be protected. You have enough on your own plate. How are you handling the situation with our newest tenants?"

I considered myself dismissed and slid out of my seat, hitting the door with alacrity before I even drew breath.

CHAPTER NINETEEN

WHERE I GIVE NICHOLAS A BIT OF HIS OWN BACK

I was still standing in the hall panting when the door opened again and Nicholas popped out.

"You!"

Nicholas laughed and took my arm, directing me to a quieter portion of the house. "Hold your tongue just a moment and then you can vent your venom. Now where are you holed up writing?"

"The Dowager's morning room."

Nicholas peered at me. "Wise choice dear sister."

I shook my head and gave credit where credit was due. "Wadsworth."

Nicholas nodded. "Ahh. Of course. Where would we be without him?"

I laughed. "Remember at that one Christmas Eve Party, when we crawled around under tables stealing people's glasses and drinking the champagne?"

Nicholas's eyes got wide. "How could I forget? I had the worst hangover of my life the next day."

I laughed, "You couldn't have been more than ten, how many hangovers had you had until that point?"

Nicholas shook his head. "It's still the worst one ever some twenty years later."

"I've missed you." I stopped in the hall and hugged him tightly. "But you really put me in it at dinner. And you knew you would be."

Nicholas shrugged. "True. But it was bound to come out sooner or later and now you have approval."

"So I should thank you dear brother, is that where you are going with this?"

"More or less." Nicholas grinned and flashed his dimple.

"I'll give it proper consideration and let you know."

"I'll hold my breath then."

By the time we were ensconced in my hideout, Wadsworth had ordered coffee and biscuits delivered to the room. A tray of bottles of a harder substance had appeared as well. We helped ourselves liberally.

"So, how long have you been involved with Lila?"

Nicholas burst out laughing. "You assume quite a lot."

"How else would you know she was helping me with her film connections? Or that she had film connections in the first place."

Nicholas avoided eye contact. He was swirling the liquid in his glass. "I'm not ready to run the gauntlet with father."

I almost dropped my glass. "It's serious then?"

Nicholas nodded. "You need to marry well so they can overlook the low connections of my bride."

I did drop my glass at that. "Your bride? You're married?"

"When I was home on invalid leave after Normandy, we got married very quietly."

"Normandy? As long ago as that? I am completely out of the loop then." I poured myself another drink, a double after what Nicholas had just shared. With barely a glance for the mess on the floor, I tossed a napkin over it and collapsed back in the leather chair next to Nicholas.

Nicholas smiled. "Our parents had that little party when I left, she was there. I hadn't seen her since she was all legs and teeth at Stonecroft. We wrote the whole time I was gone. And I married her quietly after Normandy."

"A big step from pen pal to marriage."

Nicholas got up and poured himself a new drink. He took a long swallow before he answered. "I lost so many mates on that day. You know what I am talking about."

I nodded.

"It seemed so stupid to let things drift when at any moment I could be dead. So I married her."

"I can't believe she didn't tell me." I shook my head. She played her part well, complaining about parties and her mother wanting to marry her off.

"I asked her not to. I thought it would be better if I explained things to you."

"I've been home months." I scoffed.

Nicholas looked sheepish. "I know. I shall have to tell father soon though. With a little luck you'll catch a Duke or at least a Baron and I can come clean before someone notices Lila is increasing."

"You're breeding? Congratulations. I am so pleased for you." My pleasure at this news vastly outweighed my surprise or perhaps I was still too stunned from the announcement of their marriage to feel shocked at a pregnancy.

"Thank you. Don't mention it to Lila though. She wants to tell you herself."

"I hate to be the bearer of bad news but I will not be catching a Duke, a Baron, or even a footman this weekend. I am already spoken for in that department."

"What?" It was Nicholas's turn to suffer a shock to the system. At least I let him get in a couple of drinks first to dull the emotion. "Did you get married overseas to an American flyboy?"

"No. No. He's English right enough. He's the reason I am doing all this. We lost touch and this is the only way I can get back to him."

"I don't think I understand." Nicholas frowned.

"I nursed him when he got injured. Then he got transferred out with no warning and that was it. But he's an actor for Rank Films now and if I write this script then I can insist on his being cast as the male lead."

Nicholas took a long moment to respond. "I see." His voice was not joyful.

"You sound, you sound, I don't know quite what you sound but you don't sound happy for me."

Nicholas took even longer to respond this time. "I just wonder that he hasn't found you yet. That he hasn't made an effort. You cannot be hard to locate."

"What are you suggesting, Nicholas?"

"I just don't want to see you get hurt, Molly."

"What am I gaining by not risking pain? Nothing, Nicholas, nothing. You just explained this to me not five minutes ago when talking about marrying Lila. I am risking pain for the possibility of something more."

Nicholas nodded. "I don't want to fight, not with you. How can I help?"

I was somewhat mollified by his offer of assistance. "A little interference this weekend would be helpful. I am a bit of a catch so I might need a little help to avoid any unwanted tête-à-tête."

Nicholas smiled. "I can do that, much to our mother's chagrin I hope."

"That reminds me." I set down my glass and leaned forward. "When I arrived earlier today I was summoned to present myself to Mother. She was writing when I came in and she hid the letter under her blotter. I would dearly love to know who she was writing to. It might give both of us a little leverage."

"I think we need a little scheme. I know Wadsworth is trustworthy. What about Beatrice or what's the other one?"

"Alice. I think it would be better to avoid them both. Alice is already scandalized by my behavior. I think the real problem though will be mother's lady's maid. She has a nasty eye."

Nicholas considered this. "I think we will need to run interference for each other this weekend in more than one way."

I nodded and we shared a smile.

"I should let you get back to writing. I'll make your excuses downstairs." Nicholas stood and moved toward the door.

I reached out to catch his hand. "Thank you. And I am truly happy for you and Lila. I never worried that you would marry a woman I could not get along with but to have you marry such a friend." I smiled with a hint of tears in my eyes, then gave into my emotion and embraced Nicholas. He awkwardly patted my back and left as quickly as he could but sometimes one needed to offend the sensibilities of one's favorite brother. There were so few times when I could be completely myself.

CHAPTER TWENTY

WHERE I LOOK FOR MY ROSE COLORED GLASSES

After Nicholas went downstairs I tried to settle into my script, but Nicholas's concerns had taken root in the back of my mind and I found it hard to write a rosy romantic future with Patrick. I decided to turn in early, sleep well, and start at first tea. I still had two whole days and until teatime on the third to get some good words onto paper. Perhaps I could get the rough done by then and sneak time away during the weekend to polish it up into filmable shape.

Alice woke me at six with tea. I groaned but slipped into some lounging pajamas with a heavy jumper and hurried to my writing cave. Perhaps because I was still half asleep the words came easily. I wrote until Beatrice announced breakfast was served. I contemplated asking for a tray to be delivered to me but decided I should save that for lunch time. The days went quickly in this vein. I appeared for breakfast, had lunch served to me in my writing cave, and dressed for dinner. I was peppered with questions about my film script and the occasional suggestion on who should be cast in the leading roles. Nicholas of course started this conversation. He was incapable of not starting trouble when the opportunity presented itself and if the opportunity didn't present itself he employed his talent for creating it. I kept my mouth shut and gave Nicholas the evil eye often enough to remind him I could bring up uncomfortable subjects too.

Thursday afternoon found me washed, coiffed, and dressed in an appropriate but extremely expensive, courtesy of my mother, tea dress. I had thought to be in the tea room when the potential suitors arrived but my mother chastised me and sent me back upstairs to brush my hair a hundred more times and wait until I could make a suitable entrance. Nicholas kept me company at first.

"This might be a good time to go take a look around our mother's sun room."

"She is rather absorbed with the arrival of future son-in-laws." Nicholas laughed at the idea.

"Next she'll be shopping for future daughter-in-laws and won't that be a pickle for you," I teased.

Nicholas sneered at me. "I'll go downstairs."

"Use the servants' stairs."

"How will that help me? I'll just be in the kitchen and then —"

I interrupted, "Have you forgotten? If you go up a level you can use the long servants' corridor to get to the West

Wing and use those stairs to get down to the main floor almost next door to the sun room."

"Some memory you have. I had forgotten. Alright, I'm off. Wish me good hunting."

"Ugh, did you have to mention hunting?" I groaned at the thought of what the weekend would entail.

Nicholas laughed and was gone.

I tried to distract myself by writing a scene or two longhand while I waited for Alice to fetch me. How obvious would the whole mess be when the men arrived to find my whole family in residence. The smart ones probably thought it through beforehand but still the penny would drop at tea. I had worked myself into a bit of a state when Alice knocked and then entered. "My lady, her ladyship would like you to join them in the tea room."

I nodded and checked my appearance quickly before heading down. Stockings needed to be straightened yet again. Oh to live in a world without. Patrick would surely let me wear trousers after we were married.

As I entered the lounge it felt as though the entire room turned to look at me. I knew it wasn't so but certainly enough people turned to make me feel on display. I crossed to Meredith as a position of defense. She was holding a whole settee to herself with Stephen dancing attendance on her. I sat next to her and leaned in as though we did not want to be disturbed. I could occupy myself here until Nicholas came back. From across the room I caught my mother's evil eye. She pursed her lips and clearly wanted to pull me to her without being obvious. She was deep in shallow conversation with Bachelors One, Two, and Three. I would have to put my head together with Nicholas and invent some more amusing titles.

Meredith turned to me. "I don't understand why you are trying so hard to avoid this."

"I don't want to get married," I murmured through my clenched smile. I owed her an answer since she was currently granting me temporary asylum.

"Why not? Being married is delightful."

"Even to Stephen?" I muttered under my breath.

Showing a rare sense of humor Meredith smiled. "Yes, even to Stephen."

I looked at her with a dab of scrutiny. She smiled in return. I leaned back, reclining into the seat. "So, if you had to pick one…"

Meredith snickered. "That's an old game but a good one. Let's see. I don't fancy chinless men."

"That lets out half the room I think."

We laughed. I stole a quick glance at my mother. Her fury was rapidly increasing. I wondered how long till she took direct action.

Meredith asked, "What don't you like?"

"Stout men, narrow shoulders, weak lips, receding hairlines, I could go on for hours."

Meredith raised an eyebrow. "My advice is to marry a man who worships you. Marry one you can control easily and without his realizing you are running the show."

"Indeed. I'll have to see what I can do about that," I murmured, studying her out of the corner of my eye. Meredith was so much more devious than I had previously realized. Then again I had spent almost no time with her outside the family circle as it were. Clearly there were layers to her I had not appreciated.

Nicholas chose that moment to return. I patted Meredith's hand and moved to where he was waiting as Alice poured him a cup of tea. He took his time doctoring his cup, as I took my own from Alice. We moved to the far window, where I sat in the seat and Nicholas leaned against the wall next to me. "Do tell."

Nicholas smiled. "Is this really the right place to discuss this?"

"You found something then?" My pulse sped up ever so slightly.

Nicholas refused to part with the information. "How is the husband hunt proceeding?" He queried with a smirk.

"I'm avoiding mother and all men I am not related to at this time. Mother is steaming."

"You might want to move on then; I see a chinless wonder approaching."

I glanced over my shoulder. "Ahh, him. I was thinking of calling him Stout Stoat Number One."

Nicholas laughed but still slipped away. I pasted on a smile and prepared to do my duty.

I spent the next hour casually chatting and being chatted up by a variety of titled and semi-titled men my mother thought were suitable companions.

CHAPTER TWENTY ONE

WHERE I FACE INCARCERATION THEN DECIDE TO HAVE FUN WITH IT

I was grateful when it was time to dress for dinner. I had almost an hour to myself. I could write for at least half of that and then let the maid make me over in time to be suitably late for the cocktail hour. My mother, however, had other plans. I was but a minute down the hall to my writing den when I felt her catch my arm and slide hers through. She began directing our route towards the stairs up to the family suites. "Don't think you can get away that easily," she hissed under her breath and through a locked smile. "Put a smile on your face."

I complied.

As soon as we were in my room she turned on me. "How dare you behave with so little regard for my efforts and feelings."

"Perhaps I was simply behaving as my mother has taught me."

She gave a gasp and then her hand started to rise. She stopped herself before she slapped me and instead queried, "Are you implying I have shown no regard for your efforts and feelings? Do give chapter and verse."

"I told you I don't want to get married. I have told you so more than once and yet here we are with a house full of bachelors you demand I treat graciously."

"That is simply ridiculous Margaret. You are being head strong and foolish. Any woman in her right mind would be happy to be married to any one of the men I have assembled here."

"While I beg to differ, I see it will do little good. Perhaps you could more readily accept I am not in my right mind."

"Careful. If you keep up with this reckless behavior we could have you quietly tucked away in a nice relaxing sanatorium."

I was stunned. She would have me committed because I didn't want an arranged marriage? "How nice do I have to be?"

"Exceedingly."

I nodded my acquiescence. Surrender and live to fight another day I supposed.

Mother left in a whirl of self-satisfaction and finery. I sat down to write a few more scenes longhand. Sneaking down to my writing cave was not possible now; the maid would be here in mere minutes to dress me. I allowed her to talk me into a long, gossamer pale pink gown, my hair up in curls, and make up more than my usual simple mascara and lipstick. I barely looked like myself. An idea came to me while I looked at the almost stranger in the mirror. Perhaps I could pretend I was not myself. I could be the daughter my mother wanted, or at least pretend to be the daughter she imagined. Or even more fun, I could be someone different for each bachelor. I was starting to look forward to this weekend. I might need to take notes so I could remember which me was toying with which he. I laughed out loud at myself. With a flick of my curling tendrils I glided forth into battle.

At least half the guests had assembled for cocktails when I appeared. I ordered a Sidecar from the footman tending to the siphons and Tantalus. Once I had my drink I surveyed my options. Baron Fitzwater, hereafter to be known as Chinless Wonder Number One, caught my eye and nearly choked on his drink when he realized I was coming his way. I heard Nicholas chuckle from across the room and I knew this would be amusement fodder for years.

"Baron Fitzwater, so nice to finally get a chance to speak to you. I think you might have been avoiding me at tea," I trilled in a manner not unlike Lila.

"No, of course not, Lady Richmond." He hastened to correct my erroneous suggestion.

"My, aren't you formal. Call me Molly." I placed a hand on his arm.

He swallowed and stuttered, "Mmmmmm-olly."

I heard Nicholas laugh again. "Tell me all about yourself." I batted my eyelashes at him.

Still stuttering he tried to reply, "Tttthhhere's not mmmmuch to tttttell."

"Aren't you shy and retiring. You know my dear mother is keen to marry me off and if you got an invitation this weekend, you're on her short list."

Chinless Wonder Number One choked on his drink and stuttering an excuse me, left the room in a rush.

I took a short sip from my drink and surveyed the room for my next victim.

Baron Huntsford, hereafter to be referred to as Full of Courage Number One, took the bit in his mouth and crossed to me.

"Lady Margaret." He inclined his head and kissed my hand.

"Baron Huntsford, this is a pleasure."

His smile said he knew that already but was happy to hear me acknowledge the fact.

I almost couldn't decide who to be for him. I couldn't encourage him too much because he was the type to take a mile before you even gave the inch.

"I get the impression we are all here for something more than shooting this weekend."

"You get that impression do you? How quick you are." I was becoming Lila again. Hrm, maybe I would just be her all night. I could be someone else tomorrow.

Full of Courage Number One chuckled, "I do pride myself on my ability to read a situation."

I smiled and fluttered my eyelashes again.

"So Lady Richmond is fishing for a title for her lovely daughter."

"It does seem that way doesn't it. Although I don't know if a mere Barony will really do the trick. I'll have to give it some thought." With a smile, I tossed off my drink and moved on. Any longer with him and I would have needed a shower.

The attractive Earl of Manchester was sitting at the piano picking out a tune. I slid onto the bench next to him.

"What are you playing?"

"More playing at than actual playing I think but it could have been Take the A Train-Duke Ellington."

"Has it been some time since you tickled the ivories?" I added as much lilt and giggle as I could into my speech.

Giving me a long look, the Earl closed the lid to the keys. "It's been some years yes."

For a moment we locked eyes and I felt a bit of a fool playing games with this man. I decided for now he could keep his real name. "What stopped your playing?" I asked in earnest.

"The war."

"You served? In what manner?" I was instantly curious to know him better.

"Intelligence."

His answer gave me a chill. I did not want to play games with this man. I was outclassed, outmanned, and outgunned. The gong for dinner rang before I had to plan my escape.

"May I escort you in to dinner?" The Earl was unfailingly polite.

At that moment Nicholas appeared and with a smile took my arm. "I'm afraid I have that pleasure this evening, Your Lordship."

The Earl bowed his head slightly in acknowledgment. I gratefully clung to Nicholas's arm.

As soon as we got out of ear shot Nicholas whispered, "Get in over your head with that one?"

"Very much so. I need to avoid him for the rest of the weekend whenever possible."

Nicholas nodded. "I'll do what I can."

I squeezed his arm in thanks.

CHAPTER TWENTY TWO

WHERE I FORM AN ALLIANCE

Nicholas delivered me to my chair, first pulling it out for me, and then sliding it in as I sat down before he went to find his seat. To my left was Baron Guernsey, a true ride to the hounds, shooting, fishing, country land owner with probably well-cared-for tenants and a pile of stones in worse shape than Goodwin. I decided he would be known as Hunting Hound One, as he was definitely on the hunt for a rich wife.

He was clearly pleased to be seated next to me at dinner. "Good evening Lady Margaret, this is an unexpected pleasure."

I considered telling him if he was placed next to me at the first night of dinner he was considered of much lower desirability, but that might outright offend him into leaving before I got to play. I chose a polite smile instead. The chair to my right slid out and I turned to greet my right hand companion. My greeting froze in my throat. I managed to squeak out "Your Lordship, what a surprise," with considerable effort.

The Earl inclined his head. "Clearly your mother sees me as a lower value trophy."

I couldn't contain the laughter that bubbled out. "Shhhh, I don't think my other dining companion has caught on to that yet."

He leaned back in his chair to catch sight of the man on the other side of me. He snorted in response. "He would know instantly if this was a riding pack."

I cocked my head. "You really think you know people don't you."

He raised his eyebrows. "You don't want to get married."

"I've been told every woman wants to get married," I said with a grin, evading telling him he was right, yet again.

"Perhaps every other woman does but you are going out of your way to scotch every man you come in contact with."

Clearly he was not going to allow me to wiggle out of giving him his due, so I nodded my agreement.

"And since I play games better than you, I worry you." He punctuated this little gem with a sip from his wine glass and an unconcerned attitude.

I laughed again. "Touché."

My left side neighbor made a bid for my attention and I turned away from the Earl.

"Lady Margaret, tell me, do you ride to the hounds?"

My irritation at his interrupting my much more interesting conversation piqued me into volleying a greater direct hit than I had initially intended. "I think fox hunting is a barbaric institution and should be abolished."

My companion gasped and sat back in his chair as though I had physically slapped his face with my gloves.

"Don't you agree?" I asked innocently.

Baron Guernsey was almost apoplectic, "I most certainly do not." His strident voice was raised much above the constraints of proper manners. All conversations at our end of the table came to an abrupt stop as people turned to Baron Guernsey in surprise. He turned his shoulder to me very forcefully and began a conversation with the bachelor to his left.

I arranged my face into a confused puzzle and shook my head as though I didn't understand what just happened. After a moment I turned back to my right.

"That was rather a quick kill. I thought you were out to play with your victims first."

I shrugged. "He interrupted our conversation, which promised to be much more interesting."

"Lady Margaret, can I be frank with you?"

"Of course."

"I have no interest in marrying you. I am already wedded to my work."

I smiled. "Then why did you come this weekend?"

"You aren't the only one beholden to an overbearing mother."

I laughed.

"What if we joined forces to make this weekend a little less boring for both of us?"

"Why, Your Lordship, what scandalous behavior are you proposing to a young innocent such as myself?"

"You have the all the tools necessary and I have the skill. If we directed our efforts we could really make them squirm."

I sat back in my seat. I already had a partner in crime in Nicholas. Did I really want another one to complicate things? On the other hand, I could assume my spending time with the Earl would also irritate my mother given his position next to me on the first night. "I agree to the partnership with one caveat."

As he raised an eyebrow I felt just how attractive the Earl really was. I continued, "Can we toy with my mother too?"

The Earl laughed for the first time. The sound was loud and harsh and I briefly saw just how cruel his job had taught him to be. "It would be my pleasure."

"I could return the favor sometime if you liked." It seemed the polite thing to do between victims of marriage-bent mothers.

The Earl smiled. "I may take you up on that but for now we have four other bachelors to evaluate before we decide on a game plan."

I nodded. "Indeed." We plotted for the duration of the main course. By dessert we came round to my mother.

"What would really twist her other than you tetching off all the other men?"

I wrinkled my forehead in concentration. "I don't rightly know."

"Would catching me coming out of your room in the morning do it?"

I laughed startled by his suggestion. "I'm not quite willing to ruin my reputation just to irritate her."

"She would spread it around?" The Earl queried.

"People would find out, they always do."

He pondered this statement then nodded his head once in agreement.

"We'll have to think of something else. The fact that I won't be marrying any of these men should be almost enough. Just a little twist more."

"I'll keep my eyes open and see what I see."

"I suspect your eyes see rather a lot."

"That is how you stay alive in my line of work."

"Are you still *in* then?"

"Of course. Just because this war is over doesn't mean our country is safe. There is always more good work to be done."

I nodded. "I considered joining the regulars."

"What stopped you?"

I sighed, then smiled. "The same thing that usually happens to women."

"You fell in love," the Earl said with finality.

"I did."

"Then why isn't he here winning your hand publicly?"

"It's a long story. But my parents would never approve. A lowly born foot soldier in the war and now an actor. The shock and horror, can you just imagine?"

The Earl chuckled politely. "How do you plan to handle that?"

"I haven't quite worked it all out. There are complications."

"There always are. I wish you luck."

There was something in his voice that made me pause. I sussed him out to be in the same situation. "You're in love too. And it's complicated. And your family wouldn't approve," I stated with just a hint of glee in my tone.

The Earl cleared his throat. "It happens to the best of us."

My mother pushed back from the table and stood. There was only Meredith and myself to follow her to the ladies' lounge for coffee but protocol must be observed. The Earl stood and pulled out my chair for me. I thanked him with a warm smile and a hand on his. He held it for a moment too long as I walked away. I saw ire flare up in my mother's eyes. I giggled to myself.

CHAPTER TWENTY THREE

WHERE I PLAY BRIDGE WHILE BURNING A FEW BRIDGES

Once in the lounge Meredith pleaded the effort of her situation and retired to her suite. My mother was visibly pleased to have a moment to chastise me in private.

"What did you think you were doing with the Earl of Manchester?"

"Getting to know him. That's why you arranged this weekend, so I could avail myself of well bred men." I thought I sounded suitably compliant but apparently my mother disagreed.

"I do not like your tone. You can do better than the Earl."

"He made your list. I assumed you would be happy if I married any of these men."

"Some are certainly more desirable than others. I invited the Earl as a favor to his mother, who is an old friend, not because I wish to see you married to him. And I do not like to see you paying such attentions to anyone this early in the process. You will scare off the other possibilities."

I sighed. "Mother, why don't you just tell me who you want me to marry now and save us all a lot of trouble."

"Darling, I could never do that. You must choose the proper mate for yourself."

I burst out laughing, unable to contain myself.

"I do not see why you should take on so." My mother pouted.

"You clearly have an agenda, Mother. My choice not to get married isn't good enough. An Earl isn't good enough. What is good enough?"

"I can tell you what is not good enough; your attitude, young lady. I expect better of you when the men join us."

"Can you be more specific on what you want?" I asked with as much sincerity as I could muster.

"Converse with all the men. Be polite. Do not say things to shock them. Do not spend all your time with the Earl or your brother."

I nodded. Thanks for the blueprint on how to really irritate you, mother dear.

We sat in silence, drinking our coffee. My mother flipped through yet another fashion magazine which she hid quickly when the men came to join us. Tables had been set up for Bridge but we had an odd number of players. Stephen suggested it was not an issue as he would rather check on Meredith. Three tables of four were made up and it was suggested we cut for table arrangement. I drew a card that placed me with my mother, my father, and Hunting Hound One. I smiled, but then as we separated to get our drinks, I zeroed in on Chinless Wonder Number One.

"Baron Fitzgerald, I wonder if you would be so kind as to do me just the smallest of favors?"

Chinless Wonder Number One swallowed hard. "If I cccan, Lady Margaret."

"Do change seats with me. I miss my brother and would look kindly on the opportunity to spend the evening with him."

"It is my pleasure." He handed me his card and I cheerfully strode to table number one. My mother frowned when she saw how I finagled the situation to be tabled with Nicholas and the Earl of Manchester, but there was little she could do without making a scene.

As a fourth we drew Viscount Hereford's only son and heir, previously referred to as Short Stoat One. As we sat down he eyed The Earl of Manchester and said, "It appears fortune has favored us this evening. We get hours of the Lady Margaret's presence."

The Earl flicked a glance at me and with my eyes egging him on, replied, "Fate seems to favor me a bit more than you my friend. I already had the pleasure of dinner with Lady Margaret."

Nicholas choked back a laugh then caught my eye. It took him a mere moment to catch on. He didn't understand what happened at dinner but knew in that instant the Earl of Manchester and I were now in league against the other seven men.

We cut for partners and I ended up paired with the Earl. We played well together. I was beginning to see how his mind worked. It was intriguing. He anticipated my flaws and mistakes with near perfect precision allowing us to trounce the other two, whether we held the cards or not. As Nicholas and the Short Stoat moved off to the lower table, the Earl and I chatted.

"We make quite a pair Your Lordship." I raised my glass to him.

"We do indeed, Lady Margaret. Do you think I could persuade you to call me Edward?"

"I could be persuaded, if you would call me Molly."

"I bet your father hates that you use a nickname."

I laughed. "How right you are. Except of course when it suits him."

Edward cocked his head. "I am trying to imagine a situation…" He trailed off.

"I'm writing a screen play and he wishes me to use a pseudonym."

"I wouldn't have thought you a screen play writer? I suspect a further story is behind this."

I smiled but nodded my head towards our opponents who were fast approaching. And as fate would have it, it was my father and mother.

My mother looked scathingly at Edward and then turned her ire on me. I smiled innocently back at her.

My father cleared his throat and pulled out his chair. "Manchester. Margaret. I hope you are ready for a good rubber."

Edward nodded his head, "Richmond."

My father looked between Edward and I and seemed to sense we were comfortable with each other. This was not to the good as he immediately began to grill Edward as the front runner for my hand in marriage.

We shuffled and dealt as my father arranged the score pad and pen in a fidgety manner. "I do not believe you are currently occupying your seat at this time, are you Manchester?"

Edward caught my eye and I knew exactly what he was thinking. I tried not to laugh before he even responded.

"I do believe I am sitting here."

My father shook his head. "I mean in the House of Lords, Manchester. And I believe you knew that."

Edward nodded. "You are right Richmond. I did. And no, I am employing a substitute."

"Why is that?"

"I served in the war."

"The war is over and has been for some months."

Edward smiled. "My service is not over."

My father narrowed his eyes. "Are you away from home much then?"

"I am."

I was getting uncomfortable in my chair. This was getting way too close to the bone. I wanted to interrupt but I didn't know what I could possibly say to divert the conversation. My mother had been content to let the conversation roll on. She probably thought it was showing me as well as my father what a bad choice Edward was for a husband. But she did give me a way to bring things under control. "I'm sorry Mother, I didn't hear your bid."

She gave me a look that said I knew full well she hadn't bid, but my father and Edward were already giving my mother their attention. With an opening of Two No Trump we were off to a rollicking war.

CHAPTER TWENTY FOUR

WHERE I LEARN A SECRET THAT MIGHT BE OF USE

Late that evening Nicholas came to my room, creeping quietly, with a robe up over his head. "I am the ghost of Christmas present, come to bring gifts to my lady fair."

I laughed and then shushed him. "I take it this means you found something."

"Oh I found something indeed." From under his robe he produced a packet of letters tied in cliché form with a pink ribbon.

"Love letters?" I asked hopefully.

Nicholas nodded. "Between dear old mum and Lord Galwish."

"Lord Galwish." I made a face. "I always found him a little obsequious for my taste."

Nicholas assumed a puzzled look. "I always found him a little male for my taste but I'll take your word that he isn't every woman's cup of tea."

"He isn't. There's something unappetizing about him."

"You would be right." Nicholas flipped through the pile. "Read this letter."

"Ick. Do I have to?"

"I think so."

I took the letter and skimmed it with distaste. As I neared the end, I inhaled quickly. "Oh my."

Nicholas nodded.

"Am I reading this correctly? They're not only having an affair but they are indulging in-," I stopped myself.

Nicholas nodded again. "That's what I got out of that mess of filth."

I sat silent for a moment or two while my brain processed this shock. And then I realized this was the answer to both our problems in terms of our parents. "Oh Nicholas. This is wonderful."

Nicholas gaped at me for a moment. "I think you'll need to explain that one to me."

"All you need to do is tell our mother you know about her affair, that you have the letters as proof, and if she doesn't back your marriage to Lila you will not only tell our father but you will publish the more licentious portions."

"Molly, are you suggesting I blackmail our own mother?" Nicholas's horror was just a tad overdone.

"Don't pretend, dear brother, you are shocked or offended. You're just hurt I thought of it first."

"Touché." Nicholas smiled.

CHAPTER TWENTY FIVE

WHERE I PRETEND TO HUNT

Breakfast was an odd affair served buffet style at whatever time individuals rose and chose to partake. We were set to walk out with the guns at eleven and the plan was to stay out until late afternoon, partaking of a cold nuncheon served picnic style. I had no desire to shoot but thought I might steal a spare moment here and there to scribble in fun scenes. Maybe I would make my characters in the film go hunting. I donned my warmest woolen breeches and several layers of upper clothes. I topped the whole mess off with a large overcoat and knee boots to keep the mud out. Why people chose to shoot in weather like this was beyond my comprehension.

Hunting Hound One was amongst the first out the door and into the field. His face shining as crisply as the gun over his shoulder. I nudged Nicholas as he appeared next to me, whispering, "He brought his own weapon."

"But of course he did. He's after big game," Nicholas said with a flourish.

"Are you referring to me dear brother?" I replied playfully.

"You should see the size of your arse in those pants."

I slapped his arm playfully. Hunting Hound One gave me a brief look of disdain. I was clearly not taking hunting seriously enough for him or perhaps he had not yet forgiven me for my comments at dinner the night before. I smiled sweetly and was pleased to see him slightly taken aback. Further fun could be had with this one for the rest of the weekend. His gaze made its way down to my legs and he seemed mildly shocked in an unpleasant manner. His lip curled as he asked, "You ride Lady Margaret?"

"I do." I could see his mind turning. If I rode, perhaps I could be brought round to appreciate the hunt.

I slipped on my leather gloves and slid my arm through Nicholas's. As fun as toying with Hunting Hound One was, I did not want to spend the day with him. I wondered casually if Edward would join us on the field.

We walked for some time toward the woods. Nicholas was in the mood to talk. "I have decided to bring Lila down this weekend."

Startled I turned to face him. "This weekend?"

Nicholas nodded. "I rang her first thing this morning. After she dished a few choice words for waking her, she agreed to our plan. She'll be taking the train down in time for tea."

"Have you told our parents?"

"No, I had Wadsworth handle the arrangements." Nicholas laughed and I couldn't help but join in. "I plan to talk to Mother dear about her little naughty secret sometime while we are out here today. Persuade her to see things my way or at least pretend to see things my way when I come toe to toe with father."

"I applaud you. It is definitely time to be a man since you are on your way to being a father."

"Ouch, sister dear, that was uncalled for." Nicholas pressed a hand to his wounded heart in mock pain.

"Sorry, my love." I touched his cheek. "Perhaps I'm a bit jealous. I would give a good deal to be bringing Patrick here this weekend."

"You and Manchester seem to be having a good time."

"Edward is fun now that he is an ally. I think father thinks he is the front runner."

"That must please him. An Earl is no mean feat."

"I don't think so. He doesn't like that Edward is still in the military. And mother doesn't like him; she apparently only invited him because she is friends with his mother, who wants to marry him off."

Nicholas laughed. "Is this a lonely hearts club for mothers who are desperate to marry their children off?"

A male voice interrupted, "You must be talking about me."

I smiled. "Edward. We were discussing how you fail to meet my father's expectations because you don't occupy your own seat."

Nicholas laughed heartily. "Please tell me you teased him with that one."

"Just a touch but rather unsuccessfully." Edward smiled.

"He is rather a tough nut to crack."

We reached the others as they were starting to spread out into shooting formation. The games keeper was running the dogs into the underbrush in admirable style. I sat down on a bench brought along in the farm truck. Edward sat with me. "Shall we place some wagers?"

"Who will bag the most birds?" I queried, surprised at the ordinariness of his suggestion.

"I was thinking something more fun. Like who will be the first to cast aspersions on me for not shooting? Who will get the most covered in mud? Who will almost shoot a fellow hunter?"

I laughed. That sounded much more like Edward. "Ok, Hunting Hound One will be the first to cast, Chinless Wonder will end up in mud, and that one over there looking at his gun as though it might bite him will definitely almost shoot someone else."

Edward nodded sagely.

"So why aren't you shooting?"

"A bit like a busman's holiday, what?"

I looked at him for a long moment. "You shoot ducks at work then?"

Edward smiled but did not answer. I did not really expect him to though. We both wanted to back off the subject of what exactly he did at work. I made short sketches most of the morning. Edward was content to occasionally make slightly acerbic comments about the others, some of which made their way into my scene sketches. It began to hail after a few hours which I welcomed wholeheartedly. It meant we could go back to the house and I could escape into my writing cave.

CHAPTER TWENTY SIX

WHERE I ENJOY MY MOTHER'S STRUGGLE

I only emerged from the typewriter for tea because I wanted to welcome Lila when she arrived. I expected amazing fireworks when Nicholas made his announcement. I wondered if Nicholas had found time to talk to our mother yet. It would be apparent soon enough.

I hadn't changed out of my pants and sweater and decided to come down to the lounge as I was. My mother immediately sailed across the room to comment. "Darling, the least you could have done is change out of those inappropriate clothes."

I smiled. "If it's good enough for the Queen, surely its good enough for you."

I slipped out of her grasp and made for the tea urn. Once I secured a cup I headed for Edward. I did not want to waste my anticipation toying with idiots. I wanted a front row seat for the impending show.

"I'm surprised you're here with me," Edward prompted.

"There is far more entertaining sport in the offing. Just sit back and wait." I patted his hand with a smile.

The door swung open to reveal Wadsworth. In a clear voice which carried gently throughout the room he announced, "Mrs. Nicholas Leighton." He stepped to the side to allow Lila make her entrance.

My mother dropped her tea cup. So great was the shock the footman in attendance didn't even move to clear it up.

My father looked apoplectic. "What sort of joke is this?"

Nicholas crossed the room, took Lila's hand and kissed her cheek. "This is my wife Lila." The two stood there holding hands, Nicholas smiling, Lila more ethereal. She had put on a few pounds since I saw her last. I wondered just how far along she was.

My mother moved slowly across the room and held her hand out to Lila. "How charming, a surprise marriage." The smile plastered onto her face was barely millimeters out of a flat grimace.

My father clearly wanted to say more to Nicholas but his desire to maintain a noble bearing held him back. The room was still frozen in disbelief. I stood and brought Edward with me by hooking my arm in his. We crossed the room in a very public manner designed to divert some of the gaping away from my brother and his lovely wife. I kissed Lila on the cheek and introduced Edward to her.

She raised an eyebrow that told me she wanted full disclosure later. "Come and have some tea with us." I directed her across to a settee and sat with her. "Edward, darling, could you get us some tea and tasty treats?"

Nicholas gave me a look and mouthed the word "darling" at me. I contained my laughter with something approaching super human effort.

Lila leaned into me. "Who is the dashing Edward?"

"A friend; a partner in crime for the weekend."

She gave him a long appraising look as he made his way back to us with a tray full of treats. "I see."

"Put that thought out of your head Lila. I am still on the Patrick train. Riding it to the last station."

Lila laughed. "Your script must be so entertaining, if you write like you speak."

"I think I do. I mean you can only say what you know right?"

Lila cocked her head. "Oh I don't know about that. I think I could think up lies all day long."

I laughed. "Well you've certainly proved that the last couple of years."

"You know it would have been too complicated to tell you earlier. And honestly we weren't even sure this was going to work. It was a gamble and we didn't need to involve you."

"I understand. I do. And you must know how happy I am for you."

"I was planning to tell you, that Saturday you stood me up for shopping. It's your own fault that you didn't know earlier."

I laughed. "Shame, shame, shame on me."

"Nicholas would have been annoyed though. So I am glad you were too busy writing."

I slid my arm around her waist and gave her a brief squeeze. "I will be godmother, won't I?"

Lila elbowed me in the ribs. "Now you've ruined your surprise."

I laughed.

CHAPTER TWENTY SEVEN

WHERE I MOVE FORWARD ON THE GRAND PLAN

The rest of the weekend flew by in a flash. With Lila, Nicholas, and Edward running interference for me I spent little time at all with the bachelors. I snuck away to write for whole hours at a time, ably covered for by my friends and the indubitable Wadsworth. They decided not to doubly shock my parents by announcing the impending child that weekend as there were still a few months to break the news before it made itself loudly known.

Nicholas and Lila were kind enough to drive me back to London Sunday after lunch so that I was once again writing by teatime. I had liberated my father's topping new IBM typewriter out of Goodwin in my valise and set it up post haste in the library. I had a little work to finish.

Maybe a day or two. If I could be back at the Studio by Tuesday, essentially bringing the script in on the one week deadline, it might give me a touch more bargaining power.

First thing Monday morning I called Elizabeth Barrow at Rank. I let her know I was almost done; did she want the script messengered over like last time? She did. I spent the rest of the day writing, finishing in time to make afternoon tea with Lila. I had things to discuss with her.

We met at the same little Chelsea coffee house. She looked like the cat who swallowed the canary when I came in. "You are certainly happy today."

Lila smiled broadly. "Telling your parents, having them not kill either of us, really. My life is perfect."

"I can see the secret must have weighed tremendously on you."

"Nicholas and I are having supper with my parents this evening to break the good news to them."

"Will they see it as good news, then?"

Lila bubbled, "The son of an Earl? Absolutely." She paused, "Even if he is a second son."

I laughed with her.

"It will be nice to be able to live together openly. Perhaps we will get a house now."

I laughed uproariously. "How were you two keeping this quiet and still living together?"

"We took flats on the same floor in the same building. Two flats per floor. No one knows we only live in one of them." Lila giggled.

"That must have been all you. Only you could figure that out."

Lila smiled. "Nicholas is brilliant in his own way. He's thinking of training as a barrister."

This surprised me but I could see it working for him, if he could keep his sense of humor under control in the court room.

"I wanted to see you because, well, I wanted to thank you for forgiving me."

"Forgiving you for what?" I was confused. Once again the train had left me behind at the station.

"I married your favorite brother. It was a bit of a —"

I interrupted. "Lila. I love Nicholas. At the end of the day my greatest worry was that he would marry some girl I couldn't love. But I already love you. How could I be angry?"

Lila began to cry. We hugged and created a general spectacle. After we calmed down, I shared I had sent my second script off to Elizabeth and the as yet nameless director.

"You still don't know who this director is? Isn't that odd?"

"I have no idea if this is odd or not. Marlene would know. I don't know if it matters though. I expect to hear back from Elizabeth fairly quickly this time since they actually asked me to write this script."

"I hope you do. I want to know what's going to happen next." Lila was so childlike herself in many ways. She and Nicholas were a brilliant match of devilment. There would be a significant lack of the manipulative and controlling situation Meredith espoused I should find. I thought they would be happier in the long run than Meredith and Stephen.

After we finished eating and drinking, more food for Lila than for me, we walked down the street to look at Patrick's poster.

"He really is attractive. I can see why you fell for him."

"It wasn't just the eyes. He was so charming and funny."

Lila smiled. "He does sound dreamy."

I wondered briefly if she was poking fun at me.

CHAPTER TWENTY EIGHT

WHERE I GO TOE TO TOE WITH THE DIRECTOR

Wednesday afternoon Elizabeth called me and asked me to come to the studio the following day for a meeting with her and the director. I was tempted to ask if this director had a name but at this point I felt a bit silly asking. I should have done so eons ago. I would simply have to play it off when the time came.

Thursday morning I was prompt if a bit early, dressed in fashion rather than for business. I wanted to create the impression I was at home with myself and what I was trying to accomplish. Elizabeth did not come to get me from the office gargoyle. Yet another underling fetched me and delivered me to a conference room which already contained Elizabeth and a man. In fact, I think it was the man who questioned me so rudely at my failed audition. I wrinkled my nose. This was not a good start.

"Good morning. I'm Molly Worth."

Elizabeth tilted her head and gave me an odd look. "Thanks for coming in Molly. Cooper and I have looked over your script and we would like to discuss it with you."

I sat down and looked pointedly at Elizabeth. No sense in acknowledging the rude man if he wasn't going to acknowledge me.

"Cooper feels that it might be a good vehicle. What sort of compensation are you looking for to allow us the rights to your script?"

I swallowed. I had no idea. "I hadn't much considered compensation but I do have some requests."

Elizabeth looked at Cooper and then whirled her hand in the go ahead motion.

"I would like to see Patrick Dumount cast as the male love interest. And I would like to work on the film."

Copper spoke up, "You want an acting role?"

"God, no." I sounded more vehement than I meant to. "Maybe I could be an assistant to the director?"

Elizabeth started to explain how the power structure on a film worked but Cooper cut her off. "Sure. You can be my assistant. Elizabeth, as you brought me this script you can be the assistant director on this one."

Elizabeth looked stunned. She tried to speak but could only flap her jaw a few times and then blink her eyes at me.

"Thank you. And the casting?"

Cooper nodded reluctantly. "He is not my first choice to work with but he is box office popular right now. So, sure. We can try that."

I sighed deeply. "Then that is sufficient. Whatever you pay standard is fine."

Elizabeth tried to speak but this second blow must have been too much for her.

Cooper nodded again. "Fine. Work out the details with Elizabeth. I have some notes for you on how I would like the script reworked. Do you want to sit in on the rest of the casting or start your duties at filming time?"

I shook my head. "Filming time is fine."

Cooper's eyes narrowed. "Fine. Fine. Elizabeth will coordinate with you. Although I have to say I will be displacing a perfectly good assistant so you can fill that role at the most interesting time in an assistant's job. You might consider coming to work a bit earlier."

"Oh. I didn't think, I didn't know. Of course." His demeanor had me slightly flustered. "When do you need me?"

"It will take me a week or two to get things going. And you need to make those corrections. We'll be in touch, don't worry."

I nodded. Elizabeth's shock must be contagious. It was just now really sinking in that I was going to see Patrick. It was a done deal. I had executed a miracle and it only took me a month. A bit more than the "bit longer than a day," but what a miracle this was.

The script changes were painful. Cutting away what I though was witty repartee and adding less witty bits that satisfied Cooper's demands. At least, I hoped he would be satisfied. Elizabeth told me to be prepared to rewrite on the fly if during filming something wasn't working. I reported for duty the following Tuesday morning, taking notes during casting auditions, fetching coffee, typing memos, and generally acting as Cooper's Girl Friday. He was brusque with me most of the time. Seemingly pleased with my work but unwilling to show it in an obvious manner. Elizabeth, he worked like a dog but praised generously. I wondered at the dichotomy. Was he just angry that I finagled my way into a job? It would all be worth it when we started filming and I got to see Patrick.

CHAPTER TWENTY NINE

WHERE I START WORK ON THE FILM

I had no idea pre-production could go on so long. That's what the time before you start to film a movie is called, or so I learned very quickly. I had little time for anything but work in the long weeks that followed my coup. It felt like I would never get the actual prize for my accomplishment. But at long last we sat down to do read-throughs with the primary cast. I barely slept the night before. Up long before I needed to be. Dressed to the nines and jittery from too much coffee, I stocked the conference room with coffee, tea, and pastries to keep the talent appeased. That's how the production staff refer to the actors and actresses, as the talent. The writer in me took mild offense at this idea, after all they were only saying what I had written, so who was really the talent? But I didn't let this derail me from my primary goal. They filtered in all within a few minutes of the appointed start time. But not Patrick. I was on pins and needles. Did Cooper not cast him as the male lead? I thought I had been in all the auditions. He didn't audition male leads. Did he do it secretly? Mechanically I served refreshments to the incoming artists as my heart wept and my mind raced.

At twenty minutes after the appointed time Patrick sauntered in. I froze and stared. His smile wound its way around the room but his eyes slid right past me. I wanted to stomp my foot and shout his name. He slid into the open seat and yawned. "These early morning calls are such a drag."

Cooper tossed a script down the table to him. "Get used to it. I use all available day light when filming."

Patrick yawned again. "No calls before ten, it's inhumane."

Cooper's jaw tightened. "We can discuss this later. Since you are finally here, let's start the run-through." He turned slightly in his chair. "Molly, please note any difficult passages or sticky places in the script as we go through. We can talk about changes after we wrap."

I nodded and sat down with my copy of the script in the corner. My hand shook at I uncapped my pen. He was pretending for appearance sake. He had to be pretending. We shared so much in such an intense time. He couldn't have forgotten me, no matter how things appeared right now. I tried to ignore my inner turmoil so I could attend to my job. Focusing on the way they read my words, listening to them playing with inflection and cadence to find where their character was spot on, making notes where things didn't flow when spoken. We paused for refreshments halfway through the first read through. I wanted to rush to Patrick but I knew I was expected to man the eatery. I poured beverages and dispensed pastries while mentally willing Patrick to come over to me. When he finally did he flashed me a fifty watt smile. "And good morning to you my lovely. Coffee with cream and," he lingered over the pastry tray, "ah, an apple fritter."

I tried to smile but I could barely breathe and my hand shook as I poured the cream into his cup. Patrick noticed and his smile broadened. "Is the excitement a little too much for you?"

I plunked the cup in his hand and tried not to vomit on him. He peered at me for a long moment. "Have we met before?"

Hope surged through me. "Yes," I whispered.

"Did you used to work in that little sweet shop just down the road?"

I shook my head, unable to speak.

"Harrods, perhaps?"

Tears sprung into my eyes.

"Oh well, not important." He winked and returned to his seat whispering to the actress next to him.

I turned my back on the room in an effort to gather myself together. He thought I was a shop girl who had once served him. A shop girl. Rage bubbled up inside and I nourished that emotion. Better to be angry at him, than to get introspective here and now. Cooper calling for me, returned me to the room and I took my place at the table with hatred in my eyes and a pain in my heart.

We finished the first run-through at roughly lunch time. Cooper asked me to arrange lunch from craft services in advance so we could continue with further work. He explained sometimes it was a mistake to allow the cast to spend too much time together because friction could result, but in general the more chemistry they could build before we started filming the better the finished product would be. While the cast ate and talked amongst themselves, building their rapport, Cooper pulled me aside.

"You seem off. Is there a problem?"

I shook my head, afraid to speak.

Cooper gave me a long look. "I need you focused."

I nodded. He allowed my evasion and returned to the group, moving amongst them, squatting down next to chairs to talk to actors and actresses at their level. Elizabeth slid up next to me. "He's working the room. So many directors think they can treat the cast like paid servants. After all there would be no movie without the director. They forget you need someone to direct for there to be a movie. Coop gets it. He works them to get their best performance."

I nodded, considering this perspective. "I hadn't given it much thought."

Elizabeth smiled. "Why am I not surprised. Sometimes I wonder why you put yourself through all this when clearly you knew nothing about the business."

I shrugged, wondering quite frankly why I had put myself through all of this for a man who clearly-I cut the thought off. It was not the time to get maudlin. I could do that after we wrapped for the day.

Our second run-through took longer. The cast was finding their stride, getting into character, and working the lines and such. I took copious notes holding myself in reserve. When the room finally cleared out at the end of the day, the cast making plans with each other for dinner or heading off to plans they had made in advance, Cooper asked me to have the changes ready in the morning and I nodded from my seat at the table. Finally I had the room to myself and I cried. Long soul wracking sobs. When I finally came to my senses I realized, painfully, I had deluded myself. I had convinced myself that Patrick felt as much for me as I felt for him. That if I could just get to him, he would sweep me up into his arms and we would live happily ever after, just like my screen play. But I was a fool. Sadly a fool still in love if I was being honest with myself.

I had two choices as far as I could reckon. One, I could quit. Leave Cooper and Elizabeth a note and slink back to Goodwin with my tail between my legs. I could go to work on the family race track. Probably marry sweet Aiden. Live boringly ever after. Or two, I could stick it out here and make Patrick fall in love with me. Looking down at my annotated script through watery eyes I knew there was only one option. I gathered up my papers and personal items and headed home for the night. I spent three hours making Cooper's changes and typing the new script pages up to date. I needed to be back on the lot early so I could get the pages to the copy girl.

The next morning we began running scenes on the interior sets. With the plot of the movie running so much around the film business we could actually do most of the shooting, interior and exterior, on the Islington lot. I called Lila before the cast arrived because for once I needed advice.

"Mrs. Leighton has not yet risen," her house maid informed me.

"Then wake her. It is imperative I speak with her this morning."

The house maid hesitated.

"Now." I rarely used my Imperial Lady of the Realm voice but sometimes it was called for.

"One moment."

It was closer to three minutes before I heard Lila. "Do you have any idea what time it is? Or how foul morning sickness is?"

"Oh, Lila. I am so sorry. But it's desperate here."

"It better be given you got me out of bed before I ate my crackers. And if I were you I would make it quick. Things are precarious."

The need to explain and get advice before Lila rang off to be sick forced me to be more blunt than my sensibilities would have liked. "Patrick doesn't remember me. How do I get his attention?"

"He doesn't remember you? The cad. Drop him immediately."

"No, No, Lila. Please. Help me."

Lila sighed deeply. "Fine but know I think this is a bad idea. Some men prefer the chase. Ignore him. Be cold. Make him want to find out why you don't want him."

"I can do that. Thank you."

"Don't thank me. Wait till I fill Nicholas in on this little call. Ta."

I was left with a click in my ear and a sinking sensation. Nicholas would have a field day with this. No matter. When I prevailed in my task, he would have to fall in line.

CHAPTER THIRTY

WHERE I PREPARE MYSELF TO CATCH A TIGER BY THE TOE

I was ready with the new pages when we all met on set seventeen. I was bright and sunny, giving cheerful greetings to everyone in my path. Patrick was easy to ignore as he was once again late. By the time he arrived, I was busy once again taking notes for Cooper, and didn't have time to do more than slap him in the chest with his script changes. He grunted and quipped, "Well that was uncalled for."

Before I could even consider replying, Cooper frowned, "You're late, again. Look over the changes and get ready. I'll want you soon."

Throughout the day I laughed and chatted with all the cast, except Patrick. I was a blank slate whenever he came my way. It was a considerable strain however to maintain my façade. The first few times he didn't seem to notice. He was involved in his script or already in conversation with another cast member. At lunch I purposely went back to the office to work on call sheets and catering for the rest of the week and the next week too. I stayed away until I was sure they were working again and when I returned they were indeed rolling film. The first celluloid of the movie and I had missed the start, which gave me an odd little pang.

"And Action" the slate clacked and I could see from the information on it: title of the production, actress in the scene, scene number and take, Cooper started on the interior scenes we rehearsed that morning. Our leading lady was sitting at a dining table sipping coffee from a cup with her elbows resting on the table. She looked much prettier and more pensive than I did when the scene was reality for me. I remember feeling much more at loose end than pensive.

I slipped into the back of the set, weaving my way between cables and around cameras. From my vantage point I couldn't see Patrick so I watched the process unfolding in front of me. Cooper was leaning forward in his chair, intently focused on the actress. Elizabeth stood next to him consulting the clipboard in her arms. In front of them, the actor playing my father "entered" the dining room and started his lines questioning the leading lady.

It felt surreal watching all of this unfold, an out of body experience crossed with deja vu. I liked the way our actress seemed more in control than I remembered being and the father was somehow gentler than mine had been. Had I really written the scene this way or was Cooper directing them to make it all more appealing? I fervently wished I knew more about the film process so I understood what Cooper was doing. If I was going to make any sort of a go at this writing thing I needed a better understanding. Then

I caught myself. I wasn't going to be a writer; I was going to marry Patrick, settle down and begin producing all those grandbabies my mother so desperately wanted to say she had.

"Cut." Cooper got out of his chair. He and Elizabeth moved forward, making comments to the actress and actor on set. I wanted to follow, to hear what he was saying. I shook my head. That wasn't my overt job or my subterfuge job. I headed to the craft table to make sure it was adequately stocked. Patrick was lingering over the baked goods section.

"Well hello. Where have you been hiding all day?"

I ignored Patrick.

He reached out and caught my hand. "Lovely, did you not hear me?"

Keeping my voice as bland as possible I looked up, "I didn't realize you were addressing me."

"I don't see anyone else in the vicinity do you?"

Despite my desire to respond to his flirting, I stayed stoic. "I suppose not. What was your question?"

Flashing a grin, Patrick played through, "I forget. Why don't you come help me run my lines."

"I have duties to attend to. Excuse me." I pulled my hand back from his and moved toward Cooper's chair. He and Elizabeth were looking at the script and talking quietly amongst themselves. "Is there anything I can do for you?"

Cooper smiled warmly at me. "There you are. We started filming without you. I'm sorry you missed it."

"I am too but I have the filming schedules for your approval when you have time." I wondered briefly why he was suddenly being so kind to me.

"Give those to Elizabeth to look over. If there are any changes you two can work them out. Elizabeth knows how I like things done."

I nodded.

"For now you can stay and watch if you like. Just stay out of the way." His nod was half a question.

"Thank you and I will."

I slipped back behind their chairs and the cameras, rapt with attention.

The slate was edited to reflect the third take of this particular scene and we went again. When Cooper called cut he turned and asked what I thought.

"You've made it softer than I remember the scene being."

Cooper frowned. "What do you mean? Softer than you remember it?"

I hesitated. "Just, when I wrote this I remember thinking the father character was harsher than that and the girl more eager to avoid unpleasantness than willing to defend herself."

"I see." Cooper's tone held a note of something I couldn't quite identify but it made me worry that maybe he really did see.

Filming continued until late in the evening. When the actors finally got to quit the rest of us worked on in earnest now. I gave Elizabeth the shooting schedules I had drawn up so far and she reviewed them, returning them to me covered in red ink but I wasn't done. I sat in and took notes while Elizabeth and Cooper reviewed the dailies and decided what needed to be reshot in the upcoming days. I would need to work those scenes into the schedules I needed to redo when we were done here.

It was after one when I returned to the Grosvenor Square house. Good job I had taken the latch key as the house was asleep. I knew I soon needed to be as well. I had to be back on the set by seven, for filming began at eight. I wondered if the whole shooting process would be like this. Maybe it would be easier to sleep on the set. Surely there was a bedroom somewhere on the lot in moth balls. In the morning I drank three cups of coffee in the time I normally drank one, ate a fast bacon and egg sammie and then asked Quinten to procure me some books on making movies, cinematography, and the craft of writing that day.

The whole week went by in a whirl of little sleep, constant hurry up and then wait on the set, and momentous efforts to ignore Patrick. At least once every day he tried to lure me into conversation or into helping him in some way. I avoided every contretemps. I spent each unoccupied moment reading the large stack of books Quinten had procured for me. I was learning fast. Cooper seemed willing to help me learn as well. Elizabeth must have still credited me for her promotion because she explained what they were doing and why, whenever she could find a moment for me.

CHAPTER THIRTY ONE

WHERE I SHOW THE PAIN I FEEL EMBARRASSINGLY PUBLICLY

As the week wore on things got a little complicated. On the schedule was the scene when the male lead and the female lead meet again for the first time on the film set.

"Action." The slate clacked and the scene began.

In a conference room, our leading lady is behind a refreshments table serving coffee and tea. Patrick as the leading man looks debonair. In the scene he slides into the room, stopping stock still as his eyes alight on the leading lady. He glides across the room ignoring everyone he passes and goes straight to her.

"I didn't think I would ever see you again."

"Me either."

"I asked after you but they said you died, strafed by the Luftwaffe."

The leading lady shakes her head sadly. "That was another nurse, my friend, not me."

"I never stopped thinking about you. I tried, I tried to forget but I couldn't."

"I never bothered to try to forget."

Patrick reaches out for her hand. "We're together now though."

The leading lady smiles with tears in her eyes.

"And cut," Cooper called a quit to the scene. I knew he would turn to me in a moment and I couldn't let him see the tears streaming down my face. I turned quickly away and tried to get off the set. In my haste I caught my foot in a cable and would have fallen had a warm hand not caught my arm. Cooper was there escorting me out of the building into the anteroom.

"If only, huh?"

I shook my head. "If only what?"

"If only it had really gone that way." His voice held only the hint of a question.

I gasped and sobbed harder. "How did you know?"

He handed me his handkerchief. "It wasn't that hard. I auditioned you as an actress. I saw the first script you wrote. And then earlier this week…"

It was hard to stop crying when he was being so kind and rubbing my back in small circles.

"You think I'm an idiot don't you?" I murmured through tears.

"Maybe a little love sick but not an idiot." His eyes were kind and I knew his smile wasn't mocking me.

I sighed.

"About your first script, I think I should be honest with you now." Cooper was interrupted by the appearance of Elizabeth.

"Is she ok?" Then turning to me, Elizabeth asked, "Did you get hurt?"

"I'm fine, thank you for asking." I dried my cheeks and straightened my shoulders.

"We're reset. Do you want to shoot that one again?"

Cooper nodded. "Let's get a couple of variations of that one before we move on. Molly, why don't you go back to the office and check the schedule and make the additional arrangements we talked about."

I nodded. He was covering for me, giving me a chance to miss watching it all turn out alright on film. I quickly exited the set's anteroom before Elizabeth could ask for details about the additional arrangements which I would have to invent on the spot. I didn't feel I could invent anything at this point.

I spent the afternoon handling paperwork and avoiding the set. In the end I curled up in my chair with my back to the office and read one of the filmmaking books Quinten had procured for me. I was waiting for filming to wrap so I could apologize to Cooper for my inappropriate behavior earlier and thank him for his kindness. Most of the office had cleared out for the day when I felt a hand on the back of my chair. I turned expecting Elizabeth or maybe Cooper, only to see Patrick with an expression of concern.

I almost forgot my decision to be cool, but at the last moment I caught the words in my throat and remained calm. "How can I help you?"

"I was worried about you. You haven't been on the set all day." He sat on the edge of my desk and took my hand. "I missed your smile."

I swallowed, uncertain what to say or do next.

"Make it up to me by having dinner with me tonight."

"I don't," I paused, not sure what I wanted to say, "know if I am available."

Elizabeth's voice broke into the conversation, "You're not. We have dallies to run and a schedule to finalize."

Patrick sighed. "That's a shame. Rain check?"

I nodded, unable to speak. I was sadly disappointed.

Elizabeth gestured to the files on my desk, "Come on then, Cooper's waiting for us."

I stood and gathered the paperwork. I nodded shortly to Patrick hoping my unavailability would further entice him. I followed Elizabeth back to the screening room. I slipped into the chair just behind Cooper and leaned forward to speak with him while Elizabeth was talking to the film operator. "Cooper, I just wanted to say how sorry I am for the scene earlier and to thank you for how kind you were in the situation."

He turned slightly in his seat. "You don't need to apologize or thank me. I just wanted to help you."

"You have helped me, so much more than I can explain."

"You could try."

Before I could even begin to consider how to explain what was a very complicated situation, Elizabeth sat down in the seat next to Cooper, who turned back to face the screen. "Roll 'em."

SCRIPTING THE TRUTH

I turned on my small flashlight so I could see to make notes and adjustments to the filming schedule or script based on what Cooper wanted as he reviewed the dailies.

CHAPTER THIRTY TWO

WHERE I GIVE IN TO THE INEVITABLE

We shot on Saturday due to time constraints. Cooper needed to get this one in the can, as he reminded the cast and crew daily, if it was going to be produced in time to be considered for the PaF, Producer and Filmmakers, awards this year. The deadline was mere weeks away.

During daylight hours we shot more scenes set around the exteriors of the lot. After nightfall we moved indoors to shoot a "flashback" scene depicting how the young lovers met. It was not at all like I wrote it in the first script. In this one they met at the QAs' cocktail hour. He came as someone else's date and fell for the leading lady across the crowded room. It made better cinematic sense according to Cooper. It took quite some time to shoot what would be only two and a half minutes in the finished film.

I was puttering around the set, wrapping up a last few odds and ends. Cooper and Elizabeth had already left. We had agreed to meet for a working lunch the next day. Patrick came onto the set with his Burberry over his arm and his fedora in the other hand.

"I'm afraid Cooper has left. Can I help you with something, Mr. Dumount?"

Patrick smiled. "Yes, my dear Molly, you can." He slipped his arm through mine. "Come and dine with me. Save me from a sad and lonely meal."

I laughed in spite of myself. Patrick rolled his fedora up his arm and onto his head with a flourish.

"Alright then." I directed him back to the office so I could collect my things.

Along the way he kept his arm in mine and eventually I allowed my hand to float up to rest on his forearm. He placed his free hand onto mine with a smile. We flagged a cab right outside the studio lot and went to The Dorchester on Park Lane. Patrick flashed his pearly whites at the hostess and we had a prime table in mere minutes despite how busy it was with after opera and theater patrons seeking supper.

I wondered briefly how often he came here and how often he brought other women. I wasn't that naïve; I knew there had been women since he met me. I didn't want to think too much about them. I would rather think about our future together. I needed to remind him about our bond without coming right out and blatantly saying all that had transpired in France. The maitre d'hôtel escorted us to our table himself, another mark of Patrick's rising stardom.

Patrick ordered champagne without asking my opinion and then smiled at me as though I should be impressed. It was clear I would have to make allowances for our relationship to work in the long run. I smiled back.

"Molly, lovely Molly."

I smiled.

"I've been burning hours of time, pondering where we met before."

I giggled flirtatiously.

"It must have been something memorable for you or you wouldn't have taken on so. I've needed better than a week to persuade you to come out with me."

I took a sip of champagne as a stalling technique. "Does it really matter where we met? We're here now." I wondered if the line from the movie scene he had so recently shot would trigger a memory.

Patrick reached across the table to take my hand. "My thoughts exactly."

I gently disentangled my hand from his and picked up the menu. I needed a few moments to collect myself. I was torn between his not remembering anything from France and my determination to make this work. I had my selections long before the waiter appeared but I kept the menu up as a buffer.

Patrick ordered for both of us without asking me what I wanted. I smiled outwardly and sighed inwardly.

"So how did you become an actor?" I wanted to direct the conversation in a way that might jog his memory.

"After I got invalided out, the war office wanted to find something for me to do. I just happened to have a talent for acting which of course I have worked to enhance."

I smiled. "What did you do in the war?"

Patrick waved his hand. "Let's not discuss the war. It was a hard time for this country and we need to move forward."

I nodded and did not mention I served as well.

Patrick began holding court on how well his last two movies had done, how loved he was by the public, and how many directors wanted him to star in their next film. "After this movie, I should be able to write my own ticket for the rest of my career."

This got my attention. "You think this movie will be that good when it's done?"

"Of course it will. I may not like Cooper but everyone says he's bloody brilliant and a lock for the PaF this year."

Ah, so it wasn't my script he had faith in. That was vaguely disappointing but on some level I wondered how much his opinion really counted when he seemed to judge everything by how it affected him.

"Tell me about your childhood."

"You don't really want to hear about that. It was boring and typical. Mom at home, dad at the office, siblings, public school education." Patrick sounded like he was trying to sound blasé about the whole thing.

This didn't quite correlate with what he told me in the war but I didn't want to bring that up directly. And I didn't really want to challenge him this early in our budding relationship.

"Did you know the lead key grip is having an affair with two sisters in catering services? The rumor is he has them both up the duff."

I blinked at this euphemism and dazedly replied, "I had no idea."

For the rest of the evening Patrick regaled me with stories from previous films, rumors, gossip, and innuendo about people on our film crew. I was almost bored to distraction when he got round to Cooper and Elizabeth. "I heard they are having a torrid affair."

I shook my head. "I don't think so."

"No, they are. Why else would he promote her to Assistant Director after just a few months as his assistant? She has no connections, she has little experience, and she has no money. It makes no bloody sense. It must be love."

I puzzled over this for some time tuning out Patrick's ongoing babble. Elizabeth had looked quite surprised when Cooper promoted her. If they were involved wouldn't he have told her he was going to promote her? I assumed, at the time, the promotion was so that he could acquiesce to my demands.

I missed quite a lot of what Patrick said while I was puzzling over this Cooper and Elizabeth situation, but his request for me to join him on the dance floor brought me back to reality. I smiled in my pleasure at the anticipation of being in his arms and slid back my chair. He took my hand and spun me out onto the dance floor. It was a little flashy for my taste but I supposed an actor with an eye on his rising star needed to keep his profile up even on a late supper date.

Doris Day crooned "My Dreams Are Getting Better All the Time" as we waltzed around the floor. There was a little too much pizazz put on the motion for me to enjoy being enveloped in Patrick's arms but I allowed myself to float away with him none the less.

As the evening ended and we walked outside, Patrick flicked his fingers at the doorman who whistled for a waiting taxi. Enveloping me in a hug, Patrick kissed my cheek, "I wonder if you might like to join me for a nightcap at my place?"

I was flattered but demurred. "It's late, Patrick, and I have to be on the set quite early in the morning. Rain check for another time?" A little white lie to give myself a bit of room to allow him to chase me.

Patrick smiled, "Of course." He slid me into the back of the waiting taxi and blew me another kiss as he closed the door. He jauntily headed off down the street as I floated home.

CHAPTER THIRTY THREE

WHERE I GET TO ENJOY THE PLEASURE OF MISSING MY BELOVED ALL DAY

I met Elizabeth and Cooper in the viewing room at one o'clock Sunday afternoon. Cooper kindly ordered in from Cafe Royal, so we had excellent food to lubricate the hours of work ahead of us. We needed to review Saturday's dailies and make notes for the upcoming week. Cooper's PaF driven schedule had us done filming in just ten more working days. Elizabeth told me privately she thought that was an insane time table and she doubted he could pull it off. I didn't know enough yet to agree or disagree with her so I merely nodded.

I could watch the dailies with much more ease after last night's date. I would see Patrick again, of that much I was sure. We would find our way to a happy ending which made the film just a fun frolic rather than a rubbing of salt in my wounds.

The discussion was much livelier that afternoon than we usually had late at night after a full day of shooting. We each argued passionately for things we thought were working brilliantly or that were codswallow.

Elizabeth had left the room for a moment when we were ready to change reels. I had no idea how to work the projector so Cooper went over to handle things. I was staring at my notes when I heard the reel clang onto the floor and Cooper emitted a curse word. I rushed to where he was and picked up the reel from the floor, opening the canister and handing him the spool.

Cooper looked embarrassed and sending a dirty look to his missing right arm, gruffly said, "Damn inconvenient."

I smiled gently. "I suspect it is. Would you like to tell me how you parted ways with the right old companion?" I hoped a little humor would soothe the situation.

Cooper smiled and his answer was as humorous as my question. "An army doctor came between us."

I cocked my head. "I hadn't known you served."

Cooper nodded, seemingly unwilling to share further details.

"I was a QA but I suppose you sussed that out already from my scripts."

Cooper nodded. "I was a pilot." His voice revealed just how unwilling he was to part with even this little tidbit of information.

"So you were invalided out and came home to make films?" I pressed on.

"I had worked in the industry before the war. So when I came home, the war office put me to work making those little war effort films. Support our troops, ration your usage, turn out the lights." Cooper laughed a little at himself.

We were still standing quite close to each other and next to the film projector. Elizabeth breezed back into the room, loudly announcing she had acquired set nineteen for our use this week in addition to set seventeen so we could save time changing setups between shots. "Molly, you'll need to arrange for extra stage hands so one set of crew can prep seventeen while the other works on nineteen and vice versa."

I stepped back from Cooper. "Of course. I'll make myself a note right now." I moved quickly to my chair and started to scribble, wondering why my cheeks were so warm.

Cooper finished loading the reel and joined us. Elizabeth must have caught some undercurrent and spent a moment looking between Cooper and I as though we were a tennis match.

"Maybe I should go arrange for the extra staff now?" I tentatively enquired.

Cooper brusquely negated that idea, "Roll the film. No point in making arrangements twice."

CHAPTER THIRTY FOUR

WHERE I DEAL WITH MY FAMILY, AGAIN

I arrived home early that evening, overjoyed to have a few hours to research. Perhaps I could put some banana and honey on my hair while I was reading; it could use a little loving care given how hard I had been working the last few weeks. Quinten informed me my brother had called.

"Nicholas? Lovely, I haven't talked to him in days." I moved towards the library to return the call.

"I'm afraid not, milady. Your brother Stephen called." Quinten's voice held the tone he reserved for announcing calamities of the highest order.

I wrinkled my nose. "Stephen? What did he want?"

"He declined to say but asked that you return his call as soon as you arrived home."

I sighed, better to get it over with so I could enjoy the hours that remained. I rang through to their home. The butler apparently knew my call was expected. "One moment please."

Shortly thereafter I heard Stephen's well-modulated tones. "Margaret, thank you for calling back. I am proud to announce the birth of my first son and heir, Stephen."

"Congratulations. How are the mother and child fairing?"

"Both Meredith and the boy are in fine shape. When can we expect you?"

"Excuse me?" I was confused by his question. Had I been trapped into saying I would visit the moment the child was born? I didn't remember that being the case. In fact I didn't remember saying I would ever visit.

"When should we expect your arrival?" Stephen asked again as though I was perhaps a little dumb or slow.

"I don't know when I can get away and come down to West Sussex. We're filming six days a week right now and on the seventh I'm still working with reviewing dailies and -"

Stephen cut me off. "I would think the birth of your first nephew would be more important than that ridiculous movie you insisted upon getting involved with." His voice was no longer well-modulated. In fact, he sounded downright tetchy.

"I'm sorry you are upset by the situation but I can't just abandon the movie. They count on me to handle my responsibilities each and every day. I fill a critical role."

Stephen did not reply for a few moments. "I find your lack of family feeling very disappointing. Goodbye Margaret."

The phone clicked in my ear. I carefully set the handset back in the cradle with a sigh. I wondered how long until I got a nasty phone call from my father criticizing my lack of family feeling.

Perhaps I should tell Quinten I wasn't taking any phone calls this evening. I rang the bell.

"Quinten, tomorrow please purchase a nice baby layette in blue and green I believe, and send it to Meredith with my love. You might also include some chocolates and bubble bath for her."

"Yes, milady."

"I don't think I will be taking any more calls this evening."

Quinten nodded, "Yes, milady. Shall I serve you dinner here?" His tone was sympathetic.

"No, I'll come to the dining room. Thank you. In fifteen minutes?"

Quinten nodded and I went upstairs to freshen up and collect the film study book I was currently working my way through.

CHAPTER THIRTY FIVE

WHERE I ANTICIPATE WATCHING MY BELOVED WORK

I was thrilled to get to the lot Monday morning. I knew I would be seeing Patrick all day. Yes, we would both be working and that meant not a considerable amount of time together but still I could watch him all day and know he was mine. Cooper had other ideas however. He had me spend my day running back and forth between sets nineteen and seventeen. If he was shooting on seventeen my job was to run over to nineteen and make sure the sets got changed, the costumes were prepped, and the camera and booms were ready to be picked up at a moment's notice by the cameramen and boom operators. Not that I did any of this work myself. I was supervising almost an entire secondary crew. I caught the briefest glances of

Patrick as we switched sets. He had a warm smile for me at each meeting but made no time to exchange even a word.

We took no mid-morning break and worked through lunch. By teatime I was desperate to talk to Patrick. I snuck over to set seventeen in the middle of shooting and found Patrick at the craft services table. He had a smile for me but not much else. It felt like the moment I got there he decided he needed to be somewhere else. "Lovely to see you Molly, but I really need to run the next scene's lines. You understand." He smiled and strode away before I could even begin to formulate a reply.

After shooting wrapped for the day I looked for Patrick but he was already gone; out to supper with the leading lady according to the chap who did Patrick's hair and make-up for the movie. I was a bit concerned by this turn of events. But on the other hand, the timetable on the shooting for this film was tight and Patrick was counting on this setting his career. Getting things right with his co-star was important. I knew we would find time for each other soon.

Tuesday felt like a bad copy of Monday. I ran back and forth between sets, managing the second crew and trying to catch even a moment of time with Patrick, who was even more elusive than the day before. It was mid-afternoon when Quinten appeared on set seventeen.

"My lady." Quinten bowed slightly.

"Quinten, what are you doing here?" I was shocked at his appearance.

"I apologize for interrupting your work. Sir Nicholas bid me to find you. His wife has been taken to hospital."

I gasped. "Where?"

"St Thomas' on the Thames."

"Have you brought the car? I will be out shortly-I must explain the situation to my boss."

Quinten nodded and exited back out the door.

I rushed to set nineteen and took hold of the top of Cooper's right arm without thinking. He jerked in his seat and half-whirled on me. He only needed one look at my face before he yelled, "Cut."

I pulled him away from the crowd. "I apologize for the interruption. My sister-in-law was just rushed to hospital. She's in a delicate condition and this is too early to be the proper conclusion."

Cooper nodded. "I know. Your butler came to this set first."

I inhaled sharply.

"Take the afternoon off Lady Leighton," Cooper said with a smile.

"Thank you and I'm sorry for the subterfuge about my name."

"We can discuss that later. Go on now."

I gave him a quick kiss on the cheek without thinking about what I was doing and dashed out the door missing the look of surprise and pleasure on Cooper's face.

CHAPTER THIRTY SIX

WHERE CONFUSION ABOUNDS

Quinten drove me to the hospital in admirable style. A true London driver, he knew all the shortcuts and places to avoid. I rushed upstairs to the labor ward and found Nicholas pacing the floor.

"What happened? Is she alright? Is the baby alright?" The words tumbled out of me.

"I don't know. I was in chambers. She was dizzy and then there was blood. She called for an ambulance herself and then called me. I met her here but haven't seen the doctor yet."

"I'll wait with you." I squeezed Nicholas's hand and commenced pacing the floor in time with him.

Nicholas kept muttering to himself.

"I missed that."

"What was she doing in Petticoat Lane Market? I can't imagine it."

I laughed. "Black market goods."

Nicholas stopped short and laughed. "Of course. Of course she was."

I squeezed his hand again in reassurance.

The doctor took almost an hour to come out and find us. "Your wife is in serious condition."

Nicholas turned pale and sat down in one of the chairs.

"We have given her magnesium sulfate to stop the contractions but she must remain on complete bed rest for the duration of her pregnancy."

Nicholas nodded numbly.

"Is she in danger of-" I stopped, unable to speak the unthinkable.

"To be honest, it is a possibility. We will keep her here on the floor and monitor her closely until the unborn child can be safely birthed."

"Thank you, doctor." I shook his hand. Nicholas was still unable to speak. "May we see her?"

"Of course. The nurse will take you back. We have her in a ward room right now but as soon as she is stabilized we will be moving her to a private room."

Nicholas and I clung to each other and followed the nurse back. Lila was pale and her face was tearstained. Nicholas fell upon her, "Darling." I stepped back and tried to focus out the window to give them as much privacy as one could accomplish in a room with seven laboring mothers. When the whispering stopped I made my way to the bed.

Lila smiled up at me. "I'm in a bit of a pickle."

"So I see." I tried to smile but tears came instead.

"Will you still love me if you don't get to be a godmother?" Lila asked on the verge of a wail.

"Don't talk like that. It will all turn out alright. I have faith."

Lila smiled. "You don't have faith. You just want me to feel better. And I love you for it. But you should really work on your lying skills."

I laughed through my tears.

We waited with Lila in the crowded room for over an hour before they moved her to her own room. I stayed by her side while Nicholas went home to their apartment to bring Lila the very long list of items that she requested for her stay. It was after eight when there was a knock on the door; I called out for the unknown visitor to come in.

Cooper poked his head into the room, "Is it ok?"

I nodded. The surprise of his appearance was too much for me to speak.

"I brought you some dinner. I thought you all might want something not produced for quantity over quality."

"Not from craft services then?" I quipped, having recovered my voice.

Cooper laughed and displayed the box he was carrying in his left arm.

Lila squealed, "My favorite restaurant."

"I'm glad I went out of my way then." Cooper smiled at Lila and I think she might have swooned just a touch.

I performed introductions. "Lila Leighton this is Cooper, my boss."

Lila stopped gazing at Cooper long enough to throw me a look of confusion.

Cooper gestured with the box. "Where shall I...?"

I stood quickly and crossed to Cooper, "Let me help you."

Cooper handed me the box and extended his left hand to Lila. "Henry Northrup formally, but my friends do call me Cooper."

Lila smiled and shot me another look.

The variety of food took up a great deal of the room available but Lila was delighted and ate well of everything we placed before her. We persuaded Cooper to stay and eat with us. He entertained us with filming stories from the day. I was surprised by how interested I found myself in what had happened on the set while I was gone.

Nicholas returned before too long. He took one look around the room and quipped, "Did a restaurant explode in here while I was gone?"

Lila explained to Cooper, "This is my husband Nicholas. I sent him home to bring back half my apartment contents."

"And don't I have the aching muscles to prove it." Nicholas smiled at Cooper and extended a hand. "This must be the famous Patrick I have heard so much about."

Nicholas missed Lila shaking her head like it was on a swivel. My eyes almost fell out of their sockets. "Er, actually-"

Cooper cut smoothly into the conversation, "Sadly I am not the infamous Patrick, but Molly's lowly boss."

Nicholas shot me a look. "My apologies. I should not have assumed and you know what they say about assuming."

Cooper smiled politely. "I'll take my leave now I think. Lila, it's been a pleasure to meet you. You as well Nicholas. Molly, if you need a few extra days we can make do on the set without you."

"I thank you Cooper. I'll talk it over with Lila and Nicholas and let you know in the morning."

"Of course." He left quickly, which did not entirely relieve the tension in the room.

"That was your boss?" Nicholas gave me a face as he filled his plate.

"Yes." I wondered where he was going with this.

"And you're chasing after Patrick, who is not the guy who just brought half of the Basque Restaurant in Dover Street to your sister-in-law in hospital."

I laughed a little. "Yes. What is confusing you?"

"You, little sister. You're chasing after a cad who didn't even remember you. While you have a better man waiting in the wings."

"First of all brother o' mine. Cooper is not interested in me. Second, Patrick is not a cad."

"I find it interesting that you refute what I said about Cooper first. Face it, if you were honest with yourself, Cooper is the one who really matters to you."

I shook my head the whole time he was speaking. "You don't know what you are talking about. Patrick and I are meant to be."

"Meant to be? What drivel is that? You sound like a school girl with a crush."

A scathing reply was on the tip of my tongue when Lila interceded. "Enough you two, enough. Darling, there is clearly something behind all this for Molly. Why is it so important to you that the relationship with Patrick work out?"

I swallowed hard. The words came out in a breathless rush. "Because if Patrick and I don't end up together then I killed my best friend for nothing."

Nicholas was startled. He tried to speak but Lila silenced him with a look and a hand gesture. "Could you explain a little for those of us not in the know? Did this happen in the war?"

I nodded. "Frankie said Patrick and I were meant to be, that she had faith. I believed her."

Lila nodded. "Go on."

"I refused a ride back to hospital for Frankie and I because I thought it would be disloyal to Patrick to go with these other soldiers and then we got strafed and Frankie died."

Lila understood. "Oh honey."

Nicholas on the other hand was a man. "What hogwash. You didn't kill her. The Germans did. They killed a lot of good people."

"It was my fault we were on that road."

"Nicholas, love, I don't think this situation can be solved with logic." Lila cut Nicholas off from further commentary. "I think what Molly needs to consider is if Frankie was alive would she want you to pursue Patrick or Cooper?"

I sat stupefied and was finally forced to admit, "I have no idea."

CHAPTER THIRTY SEVEN

WHERE I GO BACK TO THE FILM LOT

Lila, Nicholas, and I had worked out a rough schedule so that everyone could more or less get their needs met. I returned to the set in the morning, extra early to take care of the work I missed yesterday, and to try to catch Cooper before the cast and crew began clambering for his attention.

"Thank you so much for last night. Lila was thrilled and I really- thank you." I put a hand on Cooper's arm.

"It was my pleasure." His voice did not hold any of the warmth of the last week and he gently but quickly pulled his arm from my hand.

"I wondered if I could have a long lunch this week. Would that impact shooting too much?"

"We can work around that."

"Thank you, I don't want to be gone from the set but Lila is my oldest friend in addition to being my sister now."

Cooper nodded.

"Is there something wrong? Something I can do for you this morning?"

Cooper gave me a long look. I wanted to go on asking questions but the words wouldn't come out. Finally he said, "I understand from what was said last night that you are seeing Patrick."

I nodded.

"I would warn you to be careful. He is not the man you think he is."

"How can you say that? You don't even know what I think."

"Molly, I don't want to hurt you but I think I have a fairly good idea of the opinions you hold. I read your first script. I know who he was supposed to be in that film. I am making your second script and I know you wrote him how you see him."

There was little I could say in response to this. So I said nothing.

Cooper clearly knew when to stop beating a dead horse and changed the subject. "Do you have today's schedule?"

I nodded and handed the papers over to him. I had a hard time looking him in the face. Why was I so bothered by his opinion? It was more than his position as my boss; that much I knew. The rest was complicated and my brain refused to delve into that region of thought. I hurried to start my duties for the day, pausing to grab a fourth cup of coffee for the morning. Patrick stepped away from where his stylist was touching up his hair to the craft services table. "Darling, there you are. I missed you yesterday."

I smiled in pure happiness. "I had a family emergency."

"So I gathered. Is everything alright?"

"My sister-in-law is in hospital and will be for some time."

"How terrible. Do you think a visit from a movie star would cheer her up?"

I laughed. "Perhaps, if we can find the time."

Patrick smiled a little uncertainly. "I have to get back to the maniac with the brushes for now but supper tonight; I don't care how late you have to stay slaving for Cooper."

I nodded and was humming "My Dreams Get Better All the Time" as I wound my way through the equipment to the door. I did a little skip and twirl as I reached the door and almost ran into Elizabeth. "You're chipper today. I take it your sister is better?"

"Thank you for asking, she will be in hospital for some time but she is out of immediate danger."

"Well I for one am glad to have you back."

"Really?" I didn't realize Elizabeth was so attached to me.

"Who do you think had to do your duties as well as her own yesterday?" Her voice was teasing but there was a hint of malice lingering as well.

"My sincerest apologies," I retorted with a laugh.

"And if you're trying to keep a low profile, having your butler come to the set sort of blew that."

With a grimace, I responded I knew. "What name did he happen to ask for?"

Elizabeth shook her head, "Your real one."

I sighed. "I was hoping to avoid that. Oh well. Nothing to be done for it now."

Elizabeth raised an eyebrow at me and then headed off to attend to her own duties.

The week sped by in a whirl of sets, filming, dailies, and schedules. I had supper with Patrick every night after we wrapped and spent a long lunch with Lila to make her time in the hospital less dreary. The only thorn in what was a charming time was Cooper's coolness towards me. I missed our warm working relationship. I had no idea how to go about getting that back. He clearly disapproved of my involvement with Patrick. I could do nothing about his opinions. I did my job carefully however and took pains not to flaunt my relationship on the set.

CHAPTER THIRTY EIGHT

WHERE THE PRODIGAL DAUGHTER COMES HOME

We drove out to Goodwin on Sunday for the christening of Stephen and Meredith's son. I had planned for us to stay for the post-christening lunch and then later tea so that Patrick could meet my parents in a more intimate setting. I didn't tell anyone I was bringing Patrick. I thought perhaps if they didn't have time to think of reasons to hate him they would be polite, at least for this visit. Patrick was keen to drive his new Morgan 4/4 Drophead Coupe although the drive took longer than the train ride would have. I wrapped my hair up in a scarf and pretended to enjoy the process of being wind whipped for several hours.

As we rolled up the drive, Patrick was taking it all in. "I had no idea the property was so extensive."

"You know who my father is."

"Yes, you were admirably honest after your servant spilled the beans for you."

I laughed by way of response. I unwound my hair, checking my face and straightening my clothes as Patrick walked around to open my door. I slipped my arm through his and gave him a reassuring smile. Oddly enough he didn't seem nervous. Certainly not like an entire swarm of bats had just hatched in his stomach as they had in mine.

We crossed the courtyard to the small church on the property, a holdover from days past. It escaped me why Meredith had chosen this small, drafty church for her son's special day. We slipped in just before the service began and took the last pew on the left. I didn't want to draw a lot of attention this early in the day. Nicholas had declined given Lila's hospitalization. For some reason, which stymied Stephen, he had never made very many friends. The church wasn't terribly full as a consequence, only those who were compelled to attend by good manners.

The service was very proper and straight laced as befitted Meredith and Stephen, but thankfully quite short. I slid out of the pew and pulled Patrick with me as soon as the service closed. I did not want to find myself trapped and making introductions in a location I couldn't control.

"Shouldn't we wait for the others?" Patrick gestured back to the church.

I shook my head. "Better to get our hands on a libation before we get cross examined." I tried to smile but my face felt frozen in apprehension. I rang the bell and Wadsworth answered with a smile I knew was for me. "Lady Margaret," he paused, "and guest."

"Good afternoon Wadsworth. This is Patrick Dumount, my friend."

Wadsworth inclined his head to Patrick in greeting. "You are the first back from the christening. Drinks have been set up in the lounge."

"Thank you Wadsworth." I handed him my coat, gloves, and scarf. Patrick handed over his coat and hat with a slight expression of distaste.

As we walked away he leaned in, "You are terribly friendly with your servants."

I was briefly taken aback by his attitude. "Wadsworth has been a friend for as long as I can remember."

My answer clearly puzzled Patrick. Perhaps it was his upbringing; the lower middle class liked the class distinction to be rigidly maintained.

I headed straight for the bar in the corner of the lounge. The footman handed me my Sidecar without asking, then turned a questioning face to Patrick, who nodded he would have the same. When we both had our drinks I faced Patrick. "Are you ready?"

"Why wouldn't I be?"

"You really aren't nervous?"

"I don't know why I should be. Yes, you have the title, but it's not as though I am a nobody."

I swallowed. I doubted my parents would see things that way.

It was but a few minutes until the guests started to filter in from the church. Not more than a dozen or so all told. My parents were among the last held up by all the hand shaking and cheek kissing at the church door.

My mother caught sight of me with Patrick and frowned before crossing directly to me.

"Margaret, welcome home." She gave Patrick a long look. "Who is your friend?"

"Mother, this is Patrick Dumount."

Patrick kissed my mother's hand. "It is a pleasure to meet you Lady Richmond."

My father fetched a cocktail and then joined the group. "Dumount did you say?"

Patrick nodded his assent.

My father made a sound of thoughtfulness. He was, however, polite enough to extend his hand to Patrick.

My mother seemed mildly embarrassed by the situation. "Margaret, I wish I had known you were bringing down a guest." She glanced sideways at the eldest son of the Marquess of Winchester.

"It was a last minute decision, I'm afraid."

My mother's smile tightened. "How was your train ride, delays? You must have gotten to the church just before the service began."

Patrick smiled. "We drove. I was dying to get my Drophead Coupe out of London and see what she could really do."

My mother nodded, slightly horrified. My father asked about engine specifications and Patrick was off lecturing about his prize beauty in detail.

My mother pulled me gently to a settee away from the gentlemen. "How could you embarrass me this way?" She hissed through a frozen smile.

"The eldest son the Marquess of Winchester was your choice, mother. I barely spoke to him at your husband hunting party."

"He is a very eligible parti. He will inherit. You would be a Marquise."

"From what I can tell he has the personality of a wet fish."

"Where did you get these romantic notions of marriage?" My mother hissed in despair.

"Not from you, mother dear. Too bad you don't hide your love letters as well as you hide the actual affair."

My mother sucked in air. "Nicholas told you. He promised."

"Who do you think told him, mother?" I asked with relish.

She swallowed. "And what do you demand for your silence?"

"To drop this ridiculous effort to marry me off to a man of your choosing."

Her lips pursed and her nostrils flared but eventually she agreed.

CHAPTER THIRTY NINE

WHERE THE WOOL IS REMOVED FROM MY EYES

I joined my father and Patrick and hoped all had been going well in my absence. Patrick was still talking about his Morgan. Wet fish was staring at the rocks in his glass, now devoid of any alcohol. Finally wet fish crossed to my mother and spoke a few words to her. I had trouble catching what he said but my mother's response was clearly audible, "Of course, I will have the car brought round for you immediately."

So wet fish was clearing out? I, for one, was thrilled to hear it. You know what they say about house guests and fish smelling after three days? Well when the house guest was a wet fish you can imagine the timeline was severely curtailed. Wet fish retired upstairs to pack as Wadsworth announced lunch. In passing my mother suggested a meal be taken up to wet fish in his room so that he would not have to board the train hungry. Wadsworth nodded while murmuring, "Just so your ladyship."

Lunch was set for twelve, so clearly Wadsworth was on top of things. I imagined a thirteenth place setting had been hurriedly added to the table arrangements and then once again removed with the impending departure of wet fish. How lucky Patrick would not be the thirteenth guest.

Wadsworth pulled out my mother's chair but Patrick seated himself without providing a similar courtesy for me. My father's eyes narrowed at this affront and then gave me a brief questioning glance.

Most of the meal passed without any trouble. Both my father and my mother were seated far enough from Patrick to have no opportunity of asking any sticky questions. Eventually however, all the guests departed. Even Meredith and Stephen took their son home shortly after the luncheon was completed. I managed to convince Patrick to come for a walk with me as the other guests were leaving and my mother was occupied with accepting congratulations for the hundredth time that day.

I directed Patrick out to the stables, wanting to check on my favorite stallion. Patrick was less than pleased. "It smells out here."

"Just like fresh hay and warm horses. Our stable hands are too well trained for anything else."

"It smells," Patrick's voice was coated in disdain.

I sighed. "I just want to check on Firebrand, my horse. Then we can walk on wherever you like."

"Fine," Patrick said peevishly.

I held a quick conversation with the groom at hand and rubbed Firebrand's nose. But I was heartily disappointed that Patrick couldn't be more accommodating to my interests.

We kept out of doors until almost teatime, returning to the house to find my parents in the lounge, waiting to begin their inquisition. Patrick sat in the spare chair opposite my father on one side, as my father had suggested by gesture. My mother was on a settee across from them. She patted the seat for me to join her but I demurred, preferring to move around the room to expend my nervous energy.

My father launched the initial volley. "So Mr. Dumount, tell me where do you hale from?"

"A little village not far outside of Coventry. You wouldn't have heard of it."

"I see. And what does your father do?"

"I'm afraid he passed on some years ago," Patrick's voice was solemn.

"Then what did he do when he was alive?"

Patrick paused. From what I remember Patrick telling me in France, his father mostly drank. His mother supported the family by cleaning houses and taking in washing. "I don't much like to talk about him, Sir. Bygones be bygones."

My father nodded and I wondered just how much he understood.

"And you, Mr. Dumount, what do you do?"

"I am an actor. I'm frankly surprised you didn't recognize my name." Injured pride was evident in his voice.

Quick to sooth him, I said, "My parents aren't much for the pictures."

"But they should be. Film is an important medium of art." Patrick sounded self-important and I hoped I could head off a lecture before he got rolling.

"I prefer art I can hang on my wall," my father replied drolly.

Patrick opened his mouth to continue the subject but I spoke quickly, "Have you been to see Lila in hospital yet?"

My mother shook her head. "We are still reeling from the news she was expecting."

I sighed, "Mother, Lila will have to be in hospital for weeks. She can use all the visitors she can get."

"I'll try to make the trip next week. I suppose I could do a little shopping while I was up in London and not completely waste the effort." Her tone implied a huge concession.

I steeled my face into a smile. "I'm sure Lila will appreciate that."

When the silence stretched long enough I was beginning to worry my father would start to grill Patrick again I enquired after his pet project, the family race track. This always set my father off on a long rambling detailing of the ins and outs since the last time I asked the question. Patrick didn't even trouble to pretend to listen after the first few minutes. I wondered if he knew he sounded just like my father when he was talking about his pet car.

As my father wound down, tea was served and I began planning in my head how to get through the rest of the meal.

"Tell me Mr. Dumount, did you serve in the war?"

"I did, Sir." Patrick's voice carried all the appropriate pride of service.

"In what capacity?" My father politely asked.

"I was a pilot, Sir. Spitfires."

My lunch lurched in my stomach. I must have misheard him. He wasn't a pilot. Why would he say he was?

"That is a dangerous job, requiring rather a high measure of bravery." My father seemed to be measuring Patrick as he said this.

"I was indeed shot down. Severe burns on my back invalided me out. That's actually how I came to be an actor. The war office wanted a hero for the face of their war time film efforts."

I bolted from the room before I lost my lunch in it. Grabbing the antique fifth century urn from the hall table, I deposited the digested remnants of my lunch. He was lying. Patrick was a liar. He wasn't a pilot. He was a foot soldier. He told me he got burned pulling his friends from a bombed building that was on fire. He probably lied about that too. Wadsworth was at my elbow, taking the urn and guiding me to the upper house maid who was waiting to escort me upstairs. As compliant as a child I allowed her to direct me to my room, remove my dress and shoes, and tuck me into bed. My mind seemed to have shut down, flooded with all the things Patrick had said that were probably lies and all the things he had done that seemed dirty and underhanded in this new clearer light. I sobbed myself to sleep a short time later unable to process all the pain.

CHAPTER FORTY

WHERE I HAVE TO STOP SCRIPTING THE TRUTH

I awoke some hours later, unsure how many had passed. A damp washcloth was on the pillow next to my face. It had clearly been applied to my forehead by a well-meaning maid and then slipped off as I tossed and turned. I considered ringing the bell but if Patrick was still in the house I didn't want him to know I was up. I slipped on a robe and crept quietly down the hall to the servants' stairs, climbing up a level to their hallway. Alice was in her room listening to records and reading a film magazine. Patrick was on the cover. My stomach flipped over once more and I hoped I had no lunch left.

"My lady." Alice jumped up as I pushed open her door the rest of the way.

"Alice, is the young man I came with still in the house?"

Alice smiled. "Patrick Dumount you mean? He is dreamy, isn't he?"

The look on my face must have spoken volumes because Alice stopped waxing poetic and got to the point. "No, milady. He left shortly after Wadsworth announced you had taken ill."

I nodded. "Thank you." I turned to go, stopping before I got to the hall. "Alice, could I trouble you for a spot of tea and some toast?"

"Of course, milady."

I nodded my thanks and returned to my room. Well, at least my mother would be thrilled not to have to pretend to approve of Patrick. This started me on a fresh lot of tears which I dried hurriedly when my mother sailed into my room unannounced. "I hear you are well enough for tea and toast in bed."

I nodded.

"Please tell me you have not joined the pudding club?"

I choked on the words and in a strangled voice replied, "No, No. Definitely not that."

"Well that is something to be thankful for then."

I nodded. I hoped this might be all she had to say to me. No such luck.

"But Margaret, that boy. It might be worth it to own up to the affair just so I do not have to see him at the dining table ever again."

"No worries on that account Mother." I tried to say his name but it wouldn't come out. "That boy and I are done."

"Well," my mother smiled brightly, "I don't know how that happened but I am thrilled to hear it. Eat your toast and drink your tea and then you can come down to a nice evening meal all freshened up."

I nodded, anything to get her to leave me to my own thoughts. After a brief knock on the door Alice entered with my toast and tea. "Thank you." As I looked down I realized she made two lots of toast. One with butter thick to the edge, as I usually had it, and one dry. I started to cry yet again.

"I'm so sorry milady, I thought maybe if you were sick dry toast was better and if not, you like it with a good thick spread of butter."

I nodded, still crying, and patted Alice's hand. My mother got up from the edge of my bed and addressing Alice said, "Come along now. Margaret has had a bit of a day. She is grateful really for your thoughtfulness." I nodded and tried to smile as they made their way out of the room.

I was tempted to remain in bed for the rest of the day but I knew I would have to own up to the mess with my father sooner or later. Better to get it over with so that I could leave early the next morning and get to the set without being too horrendously late. I splashed water on my face and tried to repair some of the ravages of hours of tears, but it was useless. Perhaps if I looked truly terrible my father would go easy on me. I slipped into a black dress; after all I was in mourning for my imagination; for the whole world I created where Patrick was a good and honorable man, a hero. I couldn't manage to escape my room without sitting through a fresh lot of tears. I settled for wiping my face clean, skipping any further adornment.

I was late to the table but my father made no comment. He had bigger fish to fry at my expense.

"I apologize for my tardiness," I mumbled quietly.

From the corner of my eye I saw my father exchange a look with my mother. He was worried, that was good. He might go a bit easier on me if he was concerned about my emotional state.

"Margaret, I think we should talk about what happened today."

I nodded.

"Have you anything to say for yourself?"

"I'm sorry," I tried tentatively.

My father sighed. "What possessed you to bring that boy here? I assume you met him on set of this film you insisted on writing and then making."

I shook my head. "I met him in the war."

"In the war? He actually served then?" My father enquired, showing just how astute he really was.

I nodded. "He wasn't a pilot though."

"When you bolted, I knew something was wrong. Patrick tried to carry it off but really he has so few social graces, the meal only went downhill from there."

I nodded. "I'm sorry."

"Margaret, you do not need to be sorry. But if you could at least tell me what you were thinking…" My father trailed off hoping I would pick up the thread.

"I convinced myself he was someone he was not."

"Yes, I quite see that. But for god's sake why?"

"It's a bit of a long story."

There was silence for a moment. When I raised my gaze from my plate, my father was giving my mother a curious look. She arose from the table murmuring something about checking on the meat course.

When we were alone, my father touched my hand and when I met his eye he nodded at me to continue.

"I fell for his charm and the idea he was a hero. He had a very convincing story of how he got injured. He probably was lying then too."

"I recognize the type. He is essentially a coward who lies to make a world he can live with. I have seen more than my fair share of them."

"Well I didn't recognize it. Then he got shipped home and I pined for him. I keep wondering how much happened and how much I invented about those days."

"So you reconnected here in London."

I nodded.

"Surely reality must have intruded on your remembrances of him?"

"I wanted to believe." I stopped speaking but my father must have known there was more to come because he waited patiently.

"There was a friend, Frankie. We went to Normandy together. She and I were closer than anyone I have ever known, closer than Nicholas and I even. I think it was the stress of the war." My last sentence was somewhat of a question.

My father nodded. "Extreme circumstances build real lasting bonds."

"I got her killed. I put her in harm's way because of Patrick. I convinced myself if I didn't make it work with Patrick, then she died for nothing."

My father said nothing for a moment. "You have not explained the circumstances but no matter what they were, your friend Frankie put herself in harm's way when she enlisted as a QA. She died in service to her country. Not for you. Certainly, not for Patrick."

I began to cry. My father slipped his handkerchief into my hand.

"You know I do not think much of Americans as a rule but Patton said 'It is foolish and wrong to mourn the men who died. Rather, we should thank God that such men lived.' Or women in this case."

With this pronouncement he left the room, leaving me alone with my ghosts as I mourned all that I had lost, real and imagined.

CHAPTER FORTY ONE

WHERE I STAND IN THE CENTER OF BRIDGES BURNING AROUND ME

I was up before the sun the next morning so I could catch the first commuter express into London. I would still be at the set later than I liked, later really than my job demanded, but there was little to be done for it. Sadly all my functional clothes were in the London house. I was forced to dress in high fashion, imminently unsuitable to a day on the set. It was gone eleven by the time I rushed onto set seventeen. Cooper had just shouted "Action" and the scene was unfolding in front of me. I crept quietly up to where Elizabeth was managing from her spot at Cooper's side.

"I'm so sorry I'm late."

Elizabeth gave me a look I was unable to read. She gave my outfit a quick once over and snorted.

"Should I be supervising the reset on nineteen?"

"I hear congratulations are in order," Elizabeth whispered with a touch of venom.

"Congratulations for what?"

Elizabeth's eyes narrowed. "Fine. Play it that way. I'm sure Cooper will want to speak with you. In the meantime, here's the schedule. Go over to nineteen and prep that. We'll be wrapping shooting in the next day or two so efficiency should be your prime watchword."

I nodded and took the paperwork she handed me. I wondered what Cooper wanted to talk to me about and why I was to be congratulated. I could only think of the PaF awards but we hadn't even finished the film yet, let alone submitted anything for consideration. Unless Cooper submitted a clip or two for early judging? Was that even possible? Once again I found myself cursing my rudimentary film knowledge and vowed to study up in my available time. Now that I wasn't chasing Patrick there would be plenty of time to study. I paused, realizing my train of thought had left the station without me. Was I going to keep on working in film without Patrick as an impetus? Yes, it appeared I was. I liked inventing stories and characters and seeing them come to life. Perhaps Cooper would keep me on as his assistant and eventually promote me as he did Elizabeth. The idea thrilled me.

I worked with renewed vigor for the rest of the morning. It was doubly difficult in my too high, too thinly-cut heels. It must have been late lunch break when Cooper came over to my set.

"My apologies for being late this morning. I was at my parents' place in Sussex and missed the last train back yesterday."

Cooper nodded.

"I'll not take time off to go see Lila today to make up the work. I know it must have been a terrible inconvenience."

Cooper stared at me for a moment. "Is there anything else you want to tell me?"

"I don't think so. Elizabeth said you had something you wanted to tell me, something that I should be congratulated for?"

"You'll forgive me if I don't congratulate you. Why don't you go see Lila, in fact spend all week with her." Cooper's tone was cold and hard.

"I don't understand." I was puzzled. Why was he so angry with me? It couldn't be just the few hours I was late.

"You're fired. Clear out immediately." Cooper turned on his heel and strode back out the door.

I stood stock still for a moment, unable to catch my breath, unable to even understand what had just happened. Slowly I sunk to my knees. I felt on the verge of tears but held them back, assisted in this feat by the super human amount of crying I had done in the last twenty-four hours. I was perhaps out of tears. That is where security found me when they came to escort me from the premises. Slumped on the floor, still clutching my clipboard, unable to speak. The entire second crew was whispering around me.

CHAPTER FORTY TWO

WHERE I MAKE A BLOODY MESS OF EVERYTHING

Standing on the pavement outside the lot, my box of personal items in my arms, I felt more at a loose end than I had ever before in my life. A taxi slid to a stop in front of me. The taxi driver got out. "Ms. Leighton?"

I nodded dumbly.

"Got a tip you might be needing a taxi." He took my box and opened the back door. "Get in ducks."

I slid into the taxi, grateful I no longer had to focus on standing, walking, and carrying the box. I could just sit and vegetate.

The taxi driver placed the box on the other side of me, then got back in and drove off.

It vaguely occurred to me, I hadn't given him a direction. But I was willing to take this ride wherever it went at this particular moment. He pulled to a stop in front of St. Thomas' Hospital, where Lila was. I suddenly realized I wanted desperately to speak to her, have her help me sort this mess out. I fumbled for my purse, rummaging for money to pay the good man.

He waved it away. "Been paid for. Tip included."

"Oh." I was stupefied. "How did you know I wanted to go here, when I didn't even know?"

The taxi driver laughed and consulted his clip board. "A Mr. Northrup. Arranged for the taxi, gave the destination, paid the bill."

"Thank you." I took my box from the seat and slid out to the pavement. My feet moved of their own volition at a rapid clip, through the lobby, into the elevator, up to the third floor, down the hall, and into Lila's room, where I dropped my box in the corner and wailed, "Oh Lila. I've made such a bloody mess of everything."

Lila placidly set down the romance book she was reading and turned her big blue eyes on my face. "You do look a fright. I wish I could ring for tea. Such a bother being in hospital."

I laughed in spite of myself. Trust Lila to focus on the lack of tea while she lay in a hospital trying to save the life of her unborn babe. She patted the side of her bed and I sat willingly.

"Tell Auntie Lila all about it, darling."

So I did. I told her the whole ugly truth about Patrick. The amazing conversation I had with my father. Then being fired by Cooper who apparently ordered me a taxi and told them to bring me to her. "I can't understand it."

"Which part? Some of it seems very straightforward. Like Patrick for example, you saw what you wanted to see. You ignored every red flag that he was not a suitable match for you and I mean that in the true sense of the phrase, not the one your mother would employ."

"I know. I get that, I do. I'm astounded by my own idiocy but I understand that part."

Lila gave me a shrewd look. "Yes, I think you do finally get that. That must have been some talk with your Father."

"It was. I think I underrate him somehow. I make him more a heavy or the bogeyman or something, than he really is."

"He's certainly been kind to me. Visits twice a week, brings up hot house fruit and chocolates and magazines."

"I had no idea. My mother said they hadn't found the time yet."

"Oh your mother hasn't, thank god." We both laughed. "Really the thought of her as mother-in-law was almost enough to put me off marrying Nicholas."

"I can see that. She would have been much worse if not for our little discovery."

"Yes that was lucky. Good job, you." Lila smiled and handed me a box of chocolates, presumably from my father.

"What I don't understand is Cooper firing me. We've been working so well together. I actually thought he might keep me on after this production as his assistant. That maybe I could work my way up, become his assistant director, and then who knows maybe direct eventually."

Lila cocked her head. "You've been bitten badly with this film making bug. Bravo."

"But, Lila, he fired me. Done. Finito. Caput."

Lila shrugged. "Of course he did."

I wanted to scream. I wanted to throttle Lila. I compromised by taking a deep breath and asking very quietly and very slowly, "Why?"

Lila sighed. "Because he's in love with you."

I hit myself in the forehead. Why did I think Lila could explain any of this? She was talking complete codswallow.

"Don't get that way. Cooper is clearly Ian what's his name from your first script."

"No, he's not." That much I knew for certain.

"Yes, he is. Go back and look at your script. Pilot who lost his right arm in a crash; check. Cooper has no right arm. Nickname of Cooper; check. And in your story he wanted to stay in touch with you."

I sat there stupefied for the third time in two days. Perhaps I didn't actually know anything I thought was true. "I don't know. There were so many pilots who got shot down. There was one who approached me at the cocktail hour once. That much happened."

"Did you meet a pilot who went by the name Cooper?"

"Probably. Maybe. I don't know." I held my head in my hands. "It's all such a jumble and to tell the truth, a lot of what happened, you try to forget as soon as it happens, otherwise it's too hard to," I paused, searching for the right word to help Lila understand when she had no basis of context, "keep functioning. And the boys need you to keep going. There is always another wounded man coming in right after the one in front of you dies." I shook my head in an effort to get free from the cobwebs of war.

"I think he loves you and is upset you took Patrick home to meet your parents."

"How would he even know that? I didn't tell anyone on the set."

"Patrick could have. Probably did. You are a bit of a catch you know." Lila said this last with a smirk.

"Yes, thank you Lila. But I would rather you didn't refer to me as the catch of the day. Someone might try to serve me with vinegar and tartare sauce."

"Didn't your mother already try that? She certainly is a bit of a Tartar," Lila quipped with a laugh.

I was too busy thinking to laugh at Lila's sense of humor. "Maybe that's what Elizabeth meant by congratulations."

"Elizabeth congratulated you?"

"This morning. I didn't understand why. And she wouldn't explain."

"You'll simply have to go back and make her explain. Or you could just tackle Patrick. Take the opportunity to tell him how little you think of him."

"I would be happy never to see his lying face again."

"His face is actually rather nice. Too bad it's the rest of him that lies so profusely." Lila sighed.

I had to laugh at this epitaph for my relationship with Patrick. "I suppose I could go see Patrick but I would rather get the story from someone unbiased, like Elizabeth."

"Will she see you or is she too loyal to Cooper?" Lila asked.

"That is an excellent question. And one we can answer right now if I may use your telephone."

Lila made a sweeping gesture. "All that is mine is yours."

"Just the telephone for now my sweet and perhaps a chocolate or two." I smiled and dialed the film set from memory. The number for set seventeen rang through to the front desk which told me they were shooting on that set right now. I rang the number for set nineteen and one of the spare crew answered.

"It's Molly and I need to speak to Elizabeth, can you fetch her for me?" I asked in my kindest voice.

"I don't know if that's such a good idea Molly."

"I know they're filming on seventeen right now but you could be super quiet and just tap her shoulder for me couldn't you?"

"Give us a moment would you?"

"I'll hold."

It was a full six minutes later that the same crew member was back on the phone. "She says to tell you she has nothing to say to you."

"Oh. Well thank you anyway. And good luck with the rest of filming."

"Molly, you should know we're going to wrap tomorrow."

"Thank you again."

I hung up and turned to Lila. "She has nothing to say to me. I suppose it didn't cross her mind I might have something to say to her."

Lila said nothing in response but I knew the vague look she had on her face. It meant in a short duration of time she would pop out with some magical solution to everything. "I've got it. You'll have to go to the set and wait out front until she comes out tonight."

"That could take hours. And it's not the best of neighborhoods."

"It's that or talk to Patrick," Lila declared with a pointed look.

I sighed. "Perhaps I could get Quinten to take me in the car. Then I wouldn't be alone. And I would at least be warm and have somewhere to sit." I laughed.

"Sounds brilliant," Lila agreed, and then after a pause continued, "Of course I thought of it." Lila smiled. "Find out what Patrick told everyone and then you can make things right."

"I hope it's that simple, Lila, I truly do." Somehow I doubted it would all unwind that smoothly. I kissed her cheek and retrieved my box.

"You will come by tomorrow and tell me how it goes won't you?"

"Yes. But do me a favor and don't let Nicholas poke too much fun at me when you tell him all the ways I have made a fool of myself lately."

Lila smiled. "I love you, you know that right? And I am not without skill. I have the benefit of my situation on my side right now."

I nodded, wondering where all this was going.

"But even I cannot stop a force of nature like your brother when he gets a good rip going."

I laughed. "Touché."

CHAPTER FORTY THREE

WHERE I AM WELL AND TRULY HUMBLED

Quinten and I found ourselves parked outside the lot that evening for hours on end. After ten, I tried ringing the bell, hoping the night watchmen had not been told my new reduced status. I had a box of pastries in my hand from the bakery we used when we were splurging and I had changed into my normal set clothes.

"Ms. Worth." The watchman's voice was cold.

"Can you let me in please, I have the late snacks for during dailies."

The man nodded. "Full marks for the effort. But I was already told you were fired this morning."

I sighed and handed him the box. "You might as well take these." I headed back to the car to wait. At some point I drifted off to sleep but Quinten was alert and woke me when he saw people exiting the lot.

I hurriedly slid out of the backseat and walked across. "Elizabeth?"

"Did you not get the message? I have nothing to say to you." Her voice was hard.

"I suppose it didn't occur to you I might have something to say to you though. Actually to ask you."

"I'm not helping you get back in Cooper's good graces."

"I just want to know why you thought I should be congratulated. Because you knew I was going to be fired? I never thought you that cruel."

Elizabeth shook her head. "I didn't know that was coming."

"Then what?" I pleaded.

"Over morning coffee Patrick told everyone about his trip to meet your family and announce your engagement."

"Our what? I am not engaged to Patrick. Nor will I ever be." I was stunned.

Elizabeth eyed me suspiciously.

"He's a liar and a fraud. I could never…" I couldn't finish my sentence, nausea was rising up.

"But you took him home?" Elizabeth was back into interrogation mode.

"I did. And then he lied about his war service, in front of me. He lied." My words could have been darts seeking to destroy. "I can never forgive that. Too many *good* men-" I stopped again abruptly.

Cooper's car had been exiting the gate and had come to a stop when he saw Elizabeth and I. He rolled down the window. "Elizabeth, would you like a ride?"

Elizabeth looked to Cooper and back to me. "I believe you." Then she crossed to the car and slid into the backseat.

With a look that I would remember a very long time, Cooper rolled the window back up. I stood for a moment, paralyzed on the pavement. Slowly I made my way back to the car and let Quinten take me home.

My dismissal was final. I felt shattered. I needed a new dream. I needed a lifetime's worth of new dreams. I had not the foggiest idea where I might find them. I would visit Lila in the morning and give her the sad update but that was as far as my plans went.

****

When I filled Lila in on the previous night's happenings, she was prosaic. "Only the dead have seen the end of war."

"I don't see what in bloody hell Plato has to do with it." I was irritated beyond belief with her this morning. Although if I was being honest, I was just irritated beyond bloody hell full stop this morning.

"Unless you plan to roll over and die, the battle is only over if you want it that way."

"If you have any more brilliant ideas, I am all ears. Short of taking out a column in the newspaper advertising I am not engaged to Patrick Dumount and never will be, I really have nothing left."

"That's not a bad idea." Lila sounded amused.

"Yes, it is." I ate a chocolate and waited for her next stroke of genius.

Lila helped herself to a chocolate and made thinking noises. This was not a good sign. She had never produced a single stroke of genius while actively thinking.

"How much longer will they keep you here?" A change of topic from my dismal affairs was very much overdue.

"A few more weeks. They want the baby to be nice and fat before they let it come screaming into the world."

"That sounds like a good idea." I was thinking. "I might go home to Goodwin for a bit. But I'll return on a moment's notice when you want me."

Lila gave me a long look. "Don't go marrying your father's pet architect in a fit of pique and depression."

I laughed. "The thought hadn't crossed my mind."

"No, but I know you. You wouldn't be happy. He's too tame for you."

"Tame? You make it sound like I am some sort of fire eater."

"Aren't you? Just a bit? You've always needed a little excitement and danger."

I was once again stopped in my tracks by Lila's uncanny ability to hit the nail on the head without even looking where she was swinging. "I'll keep your sage advice in mind."

"You better, I want Cooper for a brother-in-law and nothing else will do." Lila licked the creamy center from the chocolate she had previously bitten in half and was now gesticulating with.

"I think you might be out of luck on that but I will avoid marrying any tame pets in the next few weeks at your request." I half laughed and half felt like crying.

I kissed Lila goodbye and gave my godchild a little belly rub. I felt very close to him or her right now. Having just gambled it all and lost, I knew what it was like to have one's fate hanging by a thread of fortune. I left Lila with a smile and headed for Grosvenor Square to pack. My stay at Goodwin would be of some duration, barring any unauthorized appearance of my godchild.

CHAPTER FORTY FOUR

WHERE I LICK MY WOUNDS

I rode the train to West Sussex, striving not to think of anything at all. I watched the city, then the new suburbs, and then the countryside float by in suspended animation. I dreaded facing my mother but for once I wasn't so concerned with my father's reaction. I had the sneaking suspicion that he would view whatever I told him in the vein of our conversation Sunday.

I had accepted the idea that perhaps what happened to Frankie was just war. I had accepted more or less that I had lied to myself for quite some time about a man I had known for three days under limited circumstances. Part of me was hinting that I had clung to the idea I had built of Patrick as a way to isolate myself from further loss like Frankie's death. But I could not seem to accept the loss of the career I just begun to taste, just begun to explore. I had just begun to find myself in fact, when the map was ripped from my hands.

At least Wadsworth seemed pleased to see me. "Lady Margaret, it is a pleasure to have you back with us so soon."

"Thank you Wadsworth."

"If I may be so bold, how is your career as Molly Worth turning out?"

I smiled sadly. "It has come to an end, Wadsworth, but thank you for the loan of your name."

Wadsworth bowed slightly with an incline of his head.

"Do my parents know I have returned?" I asked resolutely.

"I took the liberty of informing them of your impending arrival at lunch."

"Thank you. I have also brought back the typewriter you procured for me when I was home for the hunting weekend. Would you be so good as to return it wherever you got it from."

"Surely you will still be needing that for your next film script."

"No more scripts for me Wadsworth. I am done as a writer."

"You'll forgive me for saying your ladyship; I think that would be a shame."

I smiled but had no further response for his belief in me.

I trailed down the hall to my father's office and after a brief knock let myself in. "I'm home."

My father looked up from the paperwork in front of him. "So I see."

I smiled. "I seem to be at loose end again. I thought perhaps you could use some help on the family racetrack project?"

My father removed his glasses and focused on me. "What happened to your film?"

I smiled sadly. "That seems to be at an end."

"Do you wish to tell me more about that or should I ignore your obvious sadness?"

In spite of myself, I laughed faintly. "Could we let that go for today? I'm a bit too raw to dissect my life any further at this time."

"Of course." There was a bit of a pause and then he continued, "I suppose you could help with some of the aspects of the racetrack although to be honest when I gave you that ultimatum some weeks back I never expected to have to follow through on it."

I laughed. "I knew you were bluffing."

My father raised his eyebrow. "You did not."

"I did, you have a tell." I exclaimed gleefully.

"I beg your pardon," my father asked with all appearance of politeness.

"When you are bluffing you fiddle with the paper in front of you."

My father looked down at his hand resting on the desk which was fingering the papers he had been reviewing when I came in. "Damn."

I laughed and to my surprise my father joined in after a moment.

I moved to the desk to look at his paperwork and he started to try to explain things to me. Not too much later my mother blew in, an ill wind in silk. "It's a fine state of affairs when I have to hear from my maid that my daughter has arrived home."

"I'm sorry." I crossed to her to kiss her on the cheek. "I came straight here to beg for a job from father."

"So your movie has gone pear shaped then?" Her voice held a note of I told you so.

I nodded silently.

"Well I cannot say I am disappointed. That idea had disaster written all over it from the start." My mother was milling around the library fingering books on tables and playing with objects d'art.

My eyes filled with tears but I didn't want to give my mother the satisfaction of seeing how much blood flowed from the wounds she inflicted.

My father's voice surprised me, "Clarice."

My mother turned to face him with an innocent startled look.

"Margaret has had a rough go of it. Let us show some compassion."

They locked eyes and after a moment my mother broke off the duel of wills and flounced from the room.

I quietly said, "Thank you."

My father acted as though we had not been interrupted and resumed his lecture on the state of the motor raceway. I gave him my full attention despite how immensely boring the subject was to me.

CHAPTER FORTY FIVE

WHERE I KILL TOO MUCH TIME

The next few weeks crept by. I developed an adult relationship with my father which was one of the only positives to come from the 'film debacle' as my mother was still referring to it. I went into London twice a week to visit Lila. She never failed to ask after her future brother-in-law as she insisted upon calling Cooper. I had no news to give. In the first week I had entertained hopes that Elizabeth would call and tell me how to get back into Cooper's good graces but as no message came from the Grosvenor Square house, hope failed me.

I seemed to spend an inordinate amount of time calling back vendors and checking quotes. Perhaps that's all I was good for under the circumstances. I went into my father's office to return some paperwork I had been working on for him. Aiden was at the main desk poring over schematics and plans, flipping between pages and scribbling maniacally.

"I didn't mean to disturb you. I just need to return these to the vendors file." I lifted the paperwork in my hand and gestured towards the desk.

"Oh, of course, fine. Fine." Aiden rubbed his forehead and left a streak of ink across it.

"You seem distressed, Aiden. Is there something I can do to help you?"

"Oh, no, Lady Margaret. I'll figure it all out."

I nodded. "You have a bit of ink on your forehead." I gestured to the same spot on my face.

He flushed in a wave as only a ginger is prone to be victimized by.

I left the room quickly to try to spare him any additional embarrassment.

****

I arrived in Lila's room laden with a flowering plant, chocolates, and three new magazines on the next of my twice weekly trips.

"Darling, how nice to see you." Lila reached for the box of chocolates. "You shouldn't have, I'm getting monstrously fat."

"I think that's the baby." I laughed.

Lila shrugged. "It's a lovely excuse anyway to eat all the chocolates I want."

"I didn't know you needed an excuse. Nicholas doesn't seem the type to keep you on a short leash."

"He doesn't but a girl has to maintain her figure to maintain her self-respect," Lila said blandly while scraping the chocolate off the bottom of a crème center to figure out which flavor the cream was.

I laughed and wondered if that was my problem. I had lost a few pounds since my multiple heartbreak fiasco. My figure was suffering and my self-respect was nonexistent. I glanced down at the way my dress was bagging, my figure might soon be nonexistent if I didn't do something about the situation. "You'd better give me one of those chocolates."

Lila gave me a long look. "I think you need more than one sweetheart. Why have you been letting yourself waste away, moldering down at Goodwin?"

I shrugged.

"It can't be just the disappointment over Patrick."

I thought for a moment. "To be honest, I think I don't much care about that anymore. I miss the film set, I miss writing, I miss working with Cooper, and Elizabeth, and the crew. I even miss the temperamental actors and the bad food from craft services."

Lila nodded. "I think you miss Cooper full stop."

I sighed. "It really doesn't matter much either way Lila. He fired me. I'm shut out of everything."

"Which upsets you more? No more film work or no more Cooper?"

"I couldn't possibly answer that. The two are intertwined completely."

"I think you could if you thought about it for more than three seconds." Lila placidly licked the cream of her next chocolate.

I sighed. "Why do you insist upon beating this horse, it's already dead."

Lila smiled. "Pregnant woman prerogative." She maintained eye contact until I agreed.

"I'll agree to give it some thought, if you agree to stop interrogating me about Cooper."

"But if I do that you won't think about it at all. I know you; you'll just pretend you don't miss him."

"Lila." I was so exasperated with her I had trouble formulating a whole sentence.

Her face contorted and her eyebrows contracted.

"Don't do that. No emotional blackmail over my life. That's not cricket."

Lila groaned, "Call the nurse."

I jumped up and rushed to the door, screaming out into the hall, "We need help."

In short duration the room was filled with medical personnel, attending to Lila and pushing me out the door. I decided to make myself useful. I scooped up my coat and rushed downstairs to fetch Nicholas from his chambers, where he was sure to be training today.

Waving wildly to flag a taxi while running down the street is a good way to get stopped by a bobby but not really guaranteed to get you a ride where you need to go. The constable who picked me up was clearly swayed by my breathless statement that my sister-in-law was having a baby and I needed to get my brother to the hospital before she delivered. Perhaps his wife had just had a baby recently or perhaps he was just kindhearted, but he quickly drove me to Nicholas's chambers.

The secretary at the outer office clearly thought I was off my rocker. Her hand stretched for the phone before I even demanded to see my brother immediately. Her indecision was obvious as her hand hovered over the phone. Would she call the police or try to talk me down herself? I didn't wait to find out. "Nicholas Leighton. Where is he?" I demanded a second time.

"Now my dear, you need to calm down."

"I am perfectly calm if slightly out of breath from running up the stairs to get here."

"You can't just storm into a barrister's chambers demanding to see the junior in residence."

"Listen you peroxide dimwit," I only got as far as that when Nicholas came out from behind one of the closed doors. "Molly." His voice registered how shocked he was to find me here insulting the office secretary.

"Nicholas, thank God. Lila is in labor."

In two quick strides he dropped the files in his arms on the secretary's desk and grabbed my hand. We were out the door in whirl. "Did you keep the taxi waiting?"

"I couldn't get one. A kind bobby gave me a lift but he had to go handle real crime I suppose."

Nicholas did a quick double-take and chuckled. "Now that is a story I want to hear, later."

I nodded. "Should we run for it or try to flag a taxi?"

"There's a stand right around the corner. We can get one there."

I nodded, grateful for Nicholas's superior knowledge of the area. We were back at the hospital in but a titch, where we paced the halls for several hours. Nicholas went in briefly to see Lila but was back in less than a minute looking decidedly dicky. "It's very," he swallowed, "there's a lot of mess in there."

I nodded.

"And Lila threw a water pitcher at me."

I laughed. "I imagine she blames you for getting her into this mess right about now. Should I go?"

Nicholas nodded gratefully and I mentally prepared myself for the surgical room. I entered quietly as not to disturb the instructions the nurse was giving Lila. I slipped around to the head of the bed and using a thoughtfully provided washcloth and basin I wiped away her sweat and tears.

Lila growled, "I hate you too right now. If we weren't friends I would never have met the demon monster who got me into this." The last words came out as a scream. I smiled and gave her my hand to squeeze. It was the least I could do given it was all my fault.

Eventually an eight pound, four ounce screaming bundle made its way into the world. Nicholas must have been listening at the door because he was in the room in a flash, shoving the staff out of the way, holding out his arms, demanding to take his son. Lila beamed at the scene and released my hand. I might have been tempted to throw something at my husband if he had the nerve to hold our child first, but Lila was an unusual woman and seemed to take pleasure in Nicholas's eagerness and joy.

I stepped out to call all the new grandparents.

My father insisted he and my mother would be on the next train. For once this pleased me. My mother would behave properly in such a public venue and my father would be thrilled to have a second grandson in as many months.

CHAPTER FORTY SIX

WHERE I GET MULTIPLE NEW HOUSEMATES

Lila and the baby had come home from the hospital to the Grosvenor Square house. My father had insisted no grandchild of his was going to be raised in an apartment with an indifferent staff. Lila had acquiesced. The comfort of a full staff was a powerful motivator, as was the beauty of the home and the abundant green walkways that surrounded it for strolling with an adorable child in a perambulator. I think the idea gained appeal when I volunteered to come and stay with her for as long as she felt she needed me.

My father did not trouble to pretend he would miss my assistance. "To be quite honest Aiden seems so distracted by your presence that the whole mess is a net negative in productivity despite all your good work."

I could see the veracity of his statements. "Lila needs company. Nicholas is already back in chambers."

"As he should be." My father hugged me briefly and I allowed him to. Quietly against my hair he said, "I shall miss you though."

This brought tears to my eyes and I nodded. I would miss him too.

Lila immediately had pictures taken of Nicholas Junior and ordered birth announcements and christening invitations. She insisted the two be sent separately and exactly one week apart from each other. For weeks it felt like all I did was address envelopes. I had paper cuts on three of my fingers and my tongue and was feeling decidedly bitter the day Meredith decided to drop in for tea and to meet the new baby, as she described him with a sniff. I think she had counted on her child being the only, and therefore spoiled, for some years.

I tried to sweep my hair into some semblance of fashion and straighten the hem on my dress as Quinten showed her into the lounge.

"Lady Margaret, what a sight you are? Is everything alright?" Meredith sounded almost shocked.

"Meredith, how lovely to see you. Everything is more or less fine. This is essentially normality."

"I see." She wrinkled her nose.

"I'm addressing envelopes practically full time now."

"I am sure there is someone you could hire for that." Meredith seemed vaguely horrified I was doing manual labor myself.

"Lila likes the personal touch and she has very specific mailing time lines all worked out. She doesn't trust anyone else to get it right."

Meredith wrinkled her nose.

"Where is my oldest nephew?" I enquired.

"With his nanny of course," Meredith responded as though the answer was obvious and I was cracked for not sussing it out myself.

"You leave him for the whole day? Doesn't he miss you?"

Meredith snorted, "I'm actually up here attending to various things and won't go home until tomorrow."

"Doesn't he need to eat?" I was gobsmacked.

"Formula is so much better for the baby," Meredith said with the air of experience two months of motherhood gave her.

I nodded, silently wondering why she thought that made sense, but felt unwilling to go ten rounds over it.

Lila breezed in with little Nich in her arms. "Meredith. Why are you here?"

I suppressed a chuckle. "Meredith came to see the baby, Lila."

Lila turned to look at Meredith. "Somehow I doubt that she much cares about babies, Molly. She didn't even bring her own with her."

Meredith bristled, "You would be wise to be persuaded to take my advice Lila; hire a quality nanny immediately. I can ask round my circle of acquaintances, perhaps another is coming available. I snapped up the one a chum from school had just finished with."

Lila shook her head.

"You'll just go on by ruining yourself, tired, cranky, covered in baby dribble."

This last comment was particularly pointed as Lila was absentmindedly picking at a bit of dried baby spit up on her shoulder.

"I don't think so." Lila seemed unperturbed.

"Don't come crying to me when Nicholas starts to look elsewhere for an attractive and intelligent mate."

"I won't." Lila continued to coo to her son and sway slowly from side to side.

I, on the other hand, had endured enough. "Meredith, perhaps you would be good enough to ring the bell for tea." I gritted my teeth and hoped I could bear the additional minutes in her sanctimonious company.

Lila reached down and snagged an invitation and an announcement with envelope from the stack I had not yet addressed, then glided out of the room with a sweet smile on her face. I wondered what she was up to.

I managed to remain polite and noncommittal with Meredith for the duration of her visit. She made it hard when she attempted to grill me over the film debacle. She kept insisting I should call Stephen and admit to him how right he was that the whole mess was a bad idea and I had come a cropper over it. I politely refused, taking a page out of Lila's book and leaving my answers at no.

CHAPTER FORTY SEVEN

WHERE I GAIN A GODSON...

Nicholas Junior's christening was held on a bright Saturday morning at St. Paul's Cathedral. Between those who came out of duty and Lila and Nicholas's friends, they more than filled the pews. The larger saucer hats adorned with feathers did not help much with the space constraints, but women will do as fashion deems.

When the priest called for the child's godparents I went to the altar alone. Nicholas and Lila had not decided on a godfather. I held the baby while the priest made pronouncements and drizzled water on his head.

Finally, the priest turned us to face the congregation and announced the blessing of Nicholas Francis Leighton. I looked quickly to Lila and she smiled and nodded. My eyes welled up with tears. I could only assume that was

Lila's good influence, memorializing someone neither she nor Nicholas had ever met, simply to please me. The congregation added their Amens to the child's blessing and we descended from the altar.

****

The beauty of full house staff when throwing a party cannot be overemphasized. I arrived back from the church before Lila and Nicholas as it was easier for me to sneak out than those carrying the prize child. But I found everything in readiness.

Entire pitchers of Pimms and Sidecars sat waiting on ice behind the bars. Bottles of gin had been opened and pour spouts installed. Glasses stood in crystal pyramids. Fresh orange juice had been squeezed by the gallon and champagne was ready to popped. I knew better than to stick my head into the kitchen and check on the food. Cook would use one of her knives on me for even insinuating by my presence that things wouldn't be at the ready when the guests arrived. Additional staff had been sent up from Goodwin.

I checked that the flowers were fresh. Nothing left but to check on my own appearance and make sure my speech was ready and on the tip of my tongue. Godmother was no easy task to fulfill.

It did not take long for the house to fill up. We overran the lounge, the library, the morning room, and the entry hall. Every space that could be filled at Number Twelve Grosvenor Square on the main floor was filled. A constant stream of servants carried treats from the kitchen through the party on silver trays. Two different bars were each manned by an efficient footman.

Lila was in her element and delighting in showing off her baby. Nicholas was delighting in showing off his stunning wife, which many had not yet met given the nature of their very secret wedding, and his beautiful son. I stood leaning by the fireplace mantel in the lounge, with a Sidecar in one hand, and the other hand on my heart. I was so happy for them I could feel the emotion straining against my chest.

Behind me a voice asked, "Does it make you want to have one?"

I turned my head, considering whether to ignore the impudent questioner when I caught sight of Cooper's face. It was wearing a hint of a smirk and for a moment I could say nothing in response. I swallowed hard. "Someday."

"How have you been?"

I laughed. Such a mundane question in light of the situation.

"Lila invited me."

"I assumed you weren't just crashing the event." I rotated my back to the wall, giving me an unfettered view of Cooper.

Cooper smiled. "I suppose I should go convey my congratulations."

"I suppose you should."

Cooper made no move to cross the room. I made no move to give him room to do so without stepping around me.

"You don't seem to be going."

"I don't, do I?" Cooper's voice held a teasing tone.

"How is our movie?" I asked in a hopeful manner.

"Our movie? You mean my movie?" Cooper teased in return.

"I wrote it," I played at indignation.

"I made it," Cooper responded in kind.

"We made it." I lifted one eye brow.

Cooper nodded. "It's done. In the can. Submitted for PaF and ready for release."

"So quick." I was a little surprised and perhaps a little hurt that Cooper could make his timeline without me.

Cooper nodded. "I needed to be done with the material."

I cocked my head to the side in a questioning manner and waited for the next thing he might say.

His gaze searched my face for something that I was not giving him. "It was good to see you."

"You too. I-" I stopped before I made a fool of myself. Once bitten, twice shy. I had made a fool of myself over Patrick too recently to put my feelings out there for ridicule again so soon.

Cooper nodded sharply and crossed the room to Lila. I watched their conversation but couldn't hear precisely what they were saying. It looked like Cooper opened with a standard congratulations. Lila demurred. Then Cooper must have said something about the baby and Lila and Lila laughed. Perhaps he commented on how attractive they both were or that Nich got his good looks from Lila. I slid a little along the wall to better my angle for trying to read their lips. Now Cooper was thanking her for the invitation and the note. What note? What had Lila said? She was touching his arm and looking at me. I quickly averted my face, drained my Sidecar, and then exited the room into the main entry hall. I could hear Lila's laughter tumble out after me.

I worked my way through the hall, around through the library, and back into the lounge through the other door. Lila was no longer talking to Cooper by then. He had helped himself to a drink, gin and tonic by the look of it, and moved off into conversation. I slipped up behind Lila, sliding my chin onto her shoulder. I whispered, "I need to talk to you."

Lila did not turn her head but I could tell she smiled because her cheek moved toward my face. "I wrote him a note telling him you were not engaged to Patrick and never had been."

I stepped back bewildered. Is that why he came today?

Lila turned around. "So go and make it all better. I want a spring wedding. I should have my figure back by then."

I shook my head. "I don't know what to say."

"Hello, I love you might be enough."

This shook me out of my reverie. "Lila. I can't say that."

Lila grinned. "But you didn't say you didn't feel that. Progress," she almost shouted gleefully.

"Shush. People will hear you."

"Look Nich needs to eat or I would go over and tell him for you. You'll just have to handle this one on your own." With a quick kiss to my cheek and a whisper to Nicholas, Lila whirled out of the room.

Nicholas looked at me, then at Cooper, and then back to me. "Looks a decent chap. He lose the arm in the war?"

I nodded.

"Actual guts then. Lila's right, marry this one." Nicholas smiled and moved to the bar to refill his drink.

I wanted to cross to Cooper then. I willed my feet to start moving. I tried to think up an opening line. But then I saw my father crossing to talk to him. My father and

Cooper in conversation and all will drained from my body. I followed Nicholas to the nearest bar.

"I think you're moving in the wrong direction, sister dear."

"I know, but look." I pursed my lips for emphasis.

Nicholas glanced over his shoulder. "Ah, dear old dad."

"Indeed." I considered the subject closed.

"I'll handle this." Nicholas strode off before I could stop him. I tossed off my drink and ordered another, sure if my father talking was to Cooper it was the fifth sign of the apocalypse, persecution. Nicholas joining them was the sixth, pure chaos. At least I could employ the seventh sign, silence, to good end here.

I slipped between the wall and a group of women complaining about their servants, in an effort to get closer to the men.

Cooper was explaining to my father, "I direct movies. Someone else writes the script usually and I tell the actors how to bring it to life. There's more to it than that but in a nut shell..."

My father nodded. "Are you associated with my daughter then?"

"Your daughter?" Cooper feigned innocence or perhaps he was stalling for time.

"Margaret." My father was having none of it.

"Ah yes, I know her as Molly, she wrote the screenplay for the last film I made," Cooper explained, matter of fact.

My father nodded and turning to Nicholas said, "Is your sister incapable of coming to a christening without bringing someone from the film world? First that actor and now this director?"

"Well dad look at it this way, she's at least moving up in the world with her taste."

Cooper cleared his throat. "I think there is some confusion. I am not –"

Nicholas interrupted Cooper. "No need to be modest about the situation Cooper. Secretly, our father is desperate to marry Molly off to someone who can keep her in line."

Cooper choked back a laugh. My father drained his glass, then looked pointedly at it, "I seem to need another drink."

Nicholas laughed heartily and then slyly beckoned to me.

I shook my head but Nicholas was having none of it.

He turned and said loudly, "Molly, there you are. Come rescue Cooper from your insane family."

My cheeks flushed red and not just from the alcohol. Cooper met my eyes and I walked towards him against my own wishes.

Nicholas slipped his arm around my waist and gave me a bit of a squeeze.

"Do you fancy a walk in the gardens?" I asked with a squeak in my voice. I cleared my throat.

Cooper nodded. "Sounds lovely."

I handed my empty again glass to Nicholas. Cooper followed suit; but before we could escape, Nicholas called out, "Lila wants a spring wedding, don't forget." I stopped breathing for a moment but somehow we continued to make our way through the throng of party goers. The outside air was bracing and while the sky was now overcast, we were blessed not to have any rain.

CHAPTER FORTY EIGHT

...AND THEN SOME

Cooper waited for me as I slipped on my gloves and carefully wound my muffler. Then he took my right hand in his left and with a twist of his wrist maneuvered my hand to be resting on his forearm as handily as if he still had both hands to work with. I gave his arm a gentle squeeze. I appreciated his deftness but knew to say so would only make him uncomfortable.

We walked in silence for at least one round of the gardens. There were things to be said but I didn't know where or even how to start. Cooper had been unfailingly kind to me but that did not mean we were anywhere near each other in the depth or type of feeling.

Finally Cooper asked, "Would you like to tell me what happened with Patrick?"

"Not particularly." I smiled. But the deafening silence after told me Cooper would need a bit more. "I finally saw what a liar he was."

"Ah."

After another lap in silence I could take it no more. "Please, just tell me straight, are you here to give me my job back or for more personal reasons?"

Cooper stopped and turned to face me, "Would you like your job back?" He sounded surprised.

"Very much so." I said with as much emphasis as I could.

"I thought you just did this movie to get close to Patrick," Cooper questioned with intensity.

"It started that way. It did. But I, I fell in love with the process. With the dynamic fluidity of it all. With the way my words drew life. It was amazing."

Cooper smiled. "You have got it bad."

"I do. I can't imagine anything more fascinating."

Cooper nodded. "Alright then. Consider yourself rehired."

"Truly?" I jumped up and down a moment before flinging my arms around him and kissing his cheek. "Oh thank you." Cooper's left arm snaked around my low back and he held me close when I tried to pull away.

"Is that all you want? To be my assistant?" Cooper asked in a low voice that vibrated through my spine.

I swallowed, "Is there another job availability in your life?"

Cooper smiled and kissed me.

When he finally released me, I was a bit dazed. Kissing Patrick had never felt like that. In fact, I don't think I ever kissed anyone who made me feel that way. Cooper took my arm again and started us in a gentle stroll back to the house.

"Did I hear correctly Lila wants a spring wedding?"

I tripped in my shock. Cooper half caught me but was so off center himself we both landed tail over tea kettle on the ground. With a laugh, we helped each other up.

"I suppose now I've well and truly fallen for you," I quipped.

Cooper laughed.

I rubbed my face. "I'm so sorry. Lila is a bit ... dramatic."

Cooper nodded. "I had noticed that, yes. What I was going to say before you so gracefully interrupted my train of thought is this: I am not a fan of spring weddings."

I nodded silently. Where was he going to go with this? Was he going to propose another time to get married? All punning aside, propose was a good word for it.

"I prefer a winter wedding. All snow and ice."

I nodded.

"I hear your mother put together a substantial weekend hunting party in a matter of weeks."

This was an odd turn of proposal. "How did you hear about that? More tales from Lila?"

Cooper laughed. "The Earl of Manchester is an old friend."

"Edward? What a small world this is?"

"We went to Eton together. Kept in touch over the years."

"I adore him, I do. If my heart wasn't otherwise engaged I think I could fall for Edward in a big way," I teased slightly hoping for a response that would give away Cooper's feelings.

"Fat lot of good that would do you." Cooper laughed heartily.

"Oh, I know he's involved with some woman his mother doesn't approve of but-" Cooper's intensifying laughter interrupted me. "Please explain the joke," I said primly.

"Darling, he's a backgammon player," Cooper said gently.

I shook my head. "What does his choice in leisure activities have to do with the price of tea in china?"

Cooper stopped in his tracks. "Oh," he exhaled in exasperation. "He's light in the pants, a pansy, a poof?"

I was more than slightly gobsmacked. "Oh." And then I began to laugh at the situation and at myself.

Once we regained our composure and began towards the house again, I said, "I suppose it's a good thing my heart is otherwise engaged then, isn't it?"

"Indeed." Cooper's tone held a hint of wry humor.

I considered how to make the next start. There were so many ways I could go and yet none of them seemed as easy as simply telling him. But Cooper didn't give me the change.

"Do you know why I didn't want to make your first screen play?"

This change of subject confused me. "Elizabeth said you thought war movies had been done."

"The script you wrote was particularly good to be honest. But I didn't want to see another actor playing me and getting shot down again, first in my plane and then during happy hour by the actress playing you." Cooper stopped walking and turned me to face him.

I shook my head. "I didn't put you in my script."

"No? So it's a mere coincidence that you have a pilot get shot down, lose his right arm, have a whole conversation about being left handed, and nickname him Cooper?" Cooper sounded almost angry with me.

I opened my mouth to speak but my brain was still puzzling out the situation. "I remember a lot of pilots. And I thought I just sort of combined them together into the archetype of the pilot who'd been shot down."

Cooper smiled. His anger seemingly evaporated. "You've been studying up? Archetype, indeed. We met. In Africa. And I wanted very much to keep in touch but you were decidedly unwilling."

"I spent most of the war avoiding romantic entanglement. I saw too many of my friends being posted for relationships with the wrong men."

Cooper nodded. "I can see that might make an impression."

"You remembered me? All those years since Africa? You remembered me?"

Cooper smiled. "Why do you think I took your script? Why do you think I let you have a job on the set? I wanted to be near you. To see if you were really the woman I remembered or if I had romanticized you into something you were not."

"So tell me then, Cooper, am I what you remembered?"

"And then some."

There was a second kiss of some duration and I leaned my head in on his shoulder when we were done, so light for want of air.

"Shall we get married at Christmas then? Or do you fancy January? It would be a wonderful excuse to go away at that time each year."

I smiled into his chest and replied, "If you have to spend Christmas with my family you might change your mind before I even get you to the front of the church."

"No danger of that."

"If we pick a date just after Christmas we could prep our next film in the meantime. We could shoot on location somewhere warm and gloriously native."

Cooper laughed. "Our next film?"

"Absolutely. I could rewrite that first script so the pilot meets her ship when she returns from war. And I was thinking, we could tell the story of more than just the one QA. Have multiple points of view."

"Is it me you love or what I can do for your film career?" Cooper asked half in jest.

"You, darling. It's always you."

Our third kiss sealed the deal.

About the Author

Transplanted from the monochromatic weather of the Silicon Valley, California with her hubby and kiddo, T.A. Henry now thrives in the rain and thunder of the Pacific Northwest. While a degree in History did not provide a lucrative career, it did teach this author how to research with the best of them. She reads non-fiction constantly and likes to use everything she absorbs as fodder for another novel.

Made in the USA
Charleston, SC
05 March 2016